Spells for the Second Sister

Nimue Brown

Copyright © Nimue Brown 2022

Cover Art by Tom Brown

Book Layout © 2022 Steam-powered Books

ISBN 9798362136420

Contents

A Few Words of Introduction
(As we are at present unknown to each other)

So here we are at the start, which is clearly not the beginning, it is just the point at which you have jumped in. You have not chosen the moment at which to wet your feet in this well. I have not chosen the point in your life at which you have discovered me, so that puts us on a passably equal footing.

I have been many people. This is manifestly not the most dramatic assertion one person has ever made to another. You have been, or will be many people, too. Taking up and putting down personas, identities, ideas and perceptions. Who we were is not who we will be. By the time you finish reading this, you will have become other than you were when we set forth together. I have never peeked ahead to see who I will be, but I could. Where, I ask, would be the fun in that?

And so we begin, at a place that is most assuredly not the beginning, but which can serve as one for now. We commence with the first life I was properly aware of.

I have been a traveller, and one who returns.

I have been a child beneath the roof of my
ancestors.

And the end of ancestral lines.

I have been a dream in a narrow valley

And flotsam tossed on uncaring waves.

I have died. I have drowned, starved,

Torn apart, bled out all existence.

And who but I could thread between

The warp and weft of all things?

Commencing Episode: 14

Everything that has gone wrong in my life recently has happened because of my grandmother. I know we aren't supposed to speak ill of the dead, but her dying has caused nothing but trouble.

So let's dive right in and test whether my therapist is lying his fat, overpaid arse off. In theory, this journal is a private 'healing space' just for me. I haven't had a whole lot of privacy recently. Or ever. But I can't talk to him in any useful way. On the whole he's a total waste of money. Not that I mind wasting my parents' money. I'm owed. But I want something for me. The therapist is not for me, he is to pacify authority and assuage guilt. This book is for me. So is telling it how it really was, as best I can, because I need to, just to get it out of my head.

My grandmother exploded. I guess that's a place to start, but it isn't the beginning. Being the unplanned, unwanted, ungood for anything unpretty, unclever unloved second child is the beginning of my life story. I guess I started wrong. Not a lot I can do about that. Not much to be said about it, either. I have not enjoyed most of my life so far.

I never was close to her. Cards from Grandmother arrived a week or two after Christmas, birthday things she sent mostly in the right month and that was about it. She hated the city, didn't visit and we never had time to visit her. So I never really knew her, and now that's she's dead, that's what bothers me the most. The things we did not do, the questions I can never ask. She's the only person who ever called me by my proper name (why give me a name and not use it?). Kathleen Sylvia West. I still haven't settled on a signature, writing it down looks awkward and funny. Kathleen. I want someone to roll my name around in their mouth and linger over it a bit. Is that too much to ask? Even at school I'm stuck with Kate. At home I am Katy-coo, but only ironically, which does not make it any better. Kathleen is an old lady name, but at least it's got a bit of dignity to it.

My parents do not believe in telling me things. I am embarrassed to say how late I found out about sex and death and why my uncle is no longer invited to parties. I think they imagine they are protecting me, but really it's themselves they are protecting. From having to talk to me. From having to come up with coherent answers and reasons. "Because I said so" is the chorus to every song my parents sing. And we're not talking 'why can't I have a pony? 'Because I said so.' We're talking why is the sky blue? Where do dust bunnies come from? We're talking questions for which 'because I said so' doesn't even make sense as an answer. For the first few years of my life, I thought my parents were gods. Why does the sun shine? Because I said so. Slowly it dawned on me that they weren't even listening to the questions. It's just the stock answer to everything, and parent-speak for 'I don't care, stop bothering me.'

Gran dying. It's a bit of a blur, to be honest. There were a lot of late night phone calls, and anxious voices. It was only through careful eavesdropping I found out about the exploding. She was in hospital, neighbours had found her and got her there. It took her a long time to die, as I remember it. The slow waiting for days, and then very suddenly it had all happened in a couple of hours at the end.

This was all a while ago and I was just getting to grips with what death means, and that no one really knows what happens and that it isn't just one of those things my parents can't be bothered to explain. I was pretty confused at the time. I don't remember the conversation clearly, but they were arguing about what she'd eaten and whether it was her fault for eating it and making herself sick in the first place. I'd not long found out about pasta, and anti-pasta, and matter and anti-matter. I may have been a bit muddled up. I mostly was as a child. They remind me of this confusion any time they think I'm being a bit thick about something. Which is often.

I'm not thick. I think about things a lot. It's just that my thoughts do not seem to line up in the kinds of straight rows other people expect. The inside of my head is like a Jackson Pollock painting. The first time I saw a piece of his, I cried, because finally I wasn't alone any more. It wasn't just me. Someone else clearly understood. I cry over things that make no sense to anyone else. This does not help me with the whole being labelled as thick issue. Weird and thick. Also, I am never going to be a child protégé and in my family, you are a gifted genius, or you are nothing.

At the funeral, I stared at her coffin the whole time, thinking about what had happened, picturing a sort of pasta, anti-pasta Granny soup on the inside. I didn't share this idea with anyone else.

Then about six months ago, Isobel went from being chess champion ballet prodigy to tennis star and model. Chess now bored her. "I just don't feel challenged by it anymore," she said, but only after a whole afternoon of door slamming, weeping and breaking things.

"You weren't even trying," our mother told her. "After all the work I've done, everything I've put into this, your biggest match, and you didn't even try!"

"You don't understand," Isobel wailed. She's good at wailing, credit where credit is due. It's a pity there are no careers in that kind of thing.

"Chess is so arid, and lifeless!"

Well yes, obviously. Had she only just noticed?

As soon as things were quiet enough that he could easily make himself heard, my father said "Well, we can't have you this unhappy. What would you like to do?" This being Dad-speak for "I hate drama, what kind of bribe must I provide to make you shut up and leave me to create in peace?" My father is an artist. His tranquillity is very important. If I had any talent for crying and screaming, I'd probably get a lot more money spent on me, too.

Apparently the ballet wasn't any fun now she could dance on the tippy tips of her toes. She worried about ruining her feet and was going to be too tall for Sadlers Wells and really, what point is there doing ballet if you aren't going to one of the top schools in the country at sixteen? Even I knew Isobel was a bit old at this point for a radical change of direction, but my mother dutifully found a really expensive tennis coach who for some reason (could it have been the money?) was totally happy to 'discover' my sister as a bound for Wimbledon natural tennis genius.

These are the scenes that reply in my mind when I can't sleep at night.

That my grandmother's now empty house was just twenty minutes by car from the club favoured by the tennis coach was just coincidence, obviously. I am not going to suggest that during my grandmother's miserable dying period, my mother was cynically picking out the guy for her next big project. There are levels of stupidity I have yet to attain. There's an art to having no idea what's going on. Like the kind of martial art where you just slide out from under the blow. I know nothing. I bend. I accept. I pretend I haven't seen, counted, figured out. I put all of it into a pot inside me, and there it smoulders.

My therapist tells me that it's perfectly normal for teenagers to feel anger towards their parents. I should not be ashamed of it. I should be willing to talk about how I feel. 'Should' is a word I despise. I don't want to share my feelings, thank you very much. I do not want to be reassured that I am normal. I want to be left alone.

My mother therefore clearly did not spend the time my grandmother was dying planning her flight from the city, and a reinvention of herself and her beloved daughter. It's all fine.

In theory my dad can work anywhere, although he needs to schmooze all the right people at regular intervals. I think he likes London. There was a post-funeral argument, in which my father muttered what I assume were his complaints, while my mother shouted 'I deserve this' at him, plus the names of other famous people who do not actually live in London. She won. She always wins. I can only assume he enjoys her explosions, because he always caves in, but never until after she's had a really good shout.

I missed the drama gene entirely. I am my father's daughter to a fair degree – anything for a quiet life. I didn't object to the plan at all – not that anyone sought my opinion. I said goodbye to all the people at school who had tolerated me. I packed my dull little life into dull little boxes and made no protests. My grandmother had exploded and now we would live in her house in the woods. In my head, it looked like something out of a Grimm's fairy tale.

It sounds romantic, doesn't it? An old house in a quiet, hidden valley. On the way in, it struck me that I could never get out of this place on my own. Not even with a pushbike. I was Luke Skywalker on Tatooine and the bright centre of the universe was someplace you could not get to from here. I've always been antisocial. I never appreciated before we left London how much more satisfying it is to be antisocial when surrounded by thousands of people who can notice how antisocial I am. I felt like an exile. Even before I got out of the car, it felt like I'd been issued with a death sentence. Here, I would no longer be a weird loner. Here, I would be alone.

It did not feel like coming home. I had no sudden sense of belonging. The place has been in Dad's family for a very long time, but I can't make that feel like anything either, even now. When we turned up, the house just seemed sad, and tired, and empty. It did not look like the fairytale image in my head, but in fairness, I had also expected to be disappointed.

"Isn't it charming!" my mother said. She'd gone mad, evidently. My mother does not go round being charmed by things, normally. Also, it wasn't charming at all. Four o'clock in the afternoon in July and the place was already in deep shade. Would it ever see any sun in winter? There were a few other grumpy looking houses nearby. Dark, heavy trees all over the place. Trees in parks are okay, but these seemed to ooze menace and I knew they didn't want me there. Yes, I do know about projection, thank you for asking. Lots of crows, or something a lot like them. Yes, I do know that people who are gloomy only see gloom. I hear that one regularly. I think its bollocks. The whole place smelled damp and decaying, and inside the house it was worse, and apparently I am not enough of a goth to really appreciate these things.

My mother bustled the whole time. Weirdly, unnaturally happy. I wanted to ask, who are you, and what have you done with the other one? I just kept hoping to wake up.

The delivery van got lost, and we couldn't contact anyone, and they couldn't contact us because my grandmother did not believe in telephones. She didn't believe in televisions, either. Somehow, she had tolerated mains electricity and water in taps, but not, it transpired, warm water out of taps. That would be going too far. That night, I slept on the floorboards of my designated bedroom, wrapped in a sturdy old blanket that smelled like an animal, and hoping I never woke up. That's the first time I can remember truly wanting to die, which is clearly an important landmark in a person's life.

Next morning, mum and Isobel were off out to meet the tennis coach. More excitement. My father had to drive straight back to London to have an important conversation with someone important. Importantly. And probably in a really expensive wine bar. I hate him. Which left me alone in my dust covered clothes, in the dusty house, with leftover sandwiches to eat and instructions to sort out the delivery men if they turned up and not to go anywhere. I wish I could say I was surprised, but this is normal for my house, even when we haven't moved into it properly yet.

It's amazing how bored and hungry you can get with just limp ham sandwiches for company, waiting for removal men to un-remove themselves. Anyone who turned up at that point would have seemed like a gift from the Gods. Three pm, the dead zone, the time of least hope. A pale and graceful red haired girl stalked down the overgrown garden and peered shamelessly through the kitchen window. I wasn't in the kitchen at the time, so I crept out the back door and went round to meet/startle her. She looked about my age, which is more than I had hoped for in the arse end of beyond.

"Have you moved in?" she asked.

"No, I'm a squatter.

She looked me up and down and said nothing for a while. Then, "I could show you around?"

I looked left, into the dark cleft of the valley, and then right towards the sloping, scrubby fields stretching to nowhere. "Did I miss anything?" I asked.

"You're from London, aren't you?" She seemed impressed and annoyed in about equal measure.

"You're from around here," I replied. Statement, not question, confirming that we were not new best friends at all.

"My mum said to invite you over for a cup of tea. Are the rest of your family here?"

I thought about the missing furniture. I thought about what my missing family would look like to this girl's mother, who could turn out to be a social worker and might decide to rescue me. More importantly, tea implied biscuits, maybe cake, and I'd long since run out of sandwiches. So I followed her to one of the squat cottages, which turned out to have a big, modern extension hidden on the back. Hot running television and a microwave. I could almost feel my grandmother's disapproval.

"Just moved in? Cup of tea?" the mother was crisp and neat like someone off a washing powder commercial. Very blonde, air of efficiency. I managed to navigate small talk with nods and odd words. I hate talking to people, but she'd got plates of fruit cake and Viennese whirls and if I had to talk to get to them, I would mumble for all I was worth.

The daughter of the house turned out to be called Violet, which is a really stupid name for someone with bright red hair. She shortened it to Vee, but in my head, she was 'Violent' already. If her crispy laundered cake distributing mother had a name, I never heard it. I presented myself as Kate. No more Katy for me. New house, new me. Maybe a bit of being taken seriously for a change.

You'd think that, in a narrow valley with only one road and no traffic, that a person couldn't fail to hear a bloody great removal van. I blame the hunger and how the long hours alone had driven me loopy. I missed the removal van, and when I finally left Vee's, the valley was nearly lost in twilight and all the boxes and furniture from the old house were piled up none too neatly in the front garden. I'd been sensible and locked the front door, of course. Like you do. There was no way I could get it all in on my own. No sign of a car. It started raining and I just couldn't take it anymore and a new sort of madness took over. I was still laughing and rolling about helplessly on the ground when the car rolled in. Cue awkward scene and much unwanted melodrama.

The shouting directed my way brought people, and caused parental red faces and embarrassed introductions involving names that did not stick to new faces for very long. The neighbours helped us move things in, and it seemed friendly and kind, and they talked about what a fantastic, one of a kind old lady my Gran had been, and one of them knew my dad when he was a boy and kept calling him 'young man' which he isn't. Hard to imagine he ever was. He doesn't like being photographed so in my head he's always looked this way with his creased face and thinning hair. If I picture him at school, he's just exactly the same but shorter and wearing kid's clothes.

There we were, all moved in and the natives didn't seem hostile, but I'd seen The Wicker Man, and Inspector Morse and Bergerac. I thought I knew about villages. The probability of being murdered seemed unreasonably high.

In a matter of days my mother had, after a series of epic temper tantrums, secured her own car. She couldn't be expected to cope out here, miles from civilization, unless she could drive herself anywhere she wanted to go, any time she felt like it. My father needed his car to go back to London for work, thus she must have her own transport. My father picked a room out to be his studio and settled into it, unpacking his vast array of kit. He's a miniaturist – which to any sensible person sounds like 'small'. What it means in practice is he has to keep up with all the latest technology, so that he can make his work ever smaller. Most of it is now meaningless to the naked eye. Last year he caved in to demands from a gallery and did some huge, stretched beyond all reason versions of his painfully small art. He fretted about it for weeks. The critics accused him of selling out, and he made a lot of money.

My father did not need to live in his dead mother's house, but I think it appealed to his idea of what an artist should be like. This matters to him. I know this because he keeps all his press cuttings and highlights the phrases he especially likes. The week we moved, an interview with him came out in a Sunday paper about how he wanted to get back to his roots, away from all the distractions of the city. "I need to earth my vision." Really, he said that. He hated the idea of coming here, and couldn't get back to London fast enough, but he likes how it looks. The whole deal could have been one big publicity stunt for him. It's not that he's superficial – he thinks about this stuff really deeply. Under that quiet and shy exterior I think there are deep pools of egotism and self-importance. Yes, I'm judging him.

Life settled down into the normal sort of family rhythm of barely seeing my father, who might or might not be in his studio, or even in the house. Man of mystery. No point asking. These days he likes to say "but of course I'd have got that for you if I'd known you wanted it." But, I'm skipping ahead. Now he feels guilty about me. Back then, I'm not sure he registered my existence at all most days. If we were in the same room it sometimes felt like he was trying very hard not to even see me.

My mother and sister were mostly out, doing important chess ballet tennis shopping. Generally life was better when they forgot about me. "You can fend for yourself, can't you?" This became my mother's only question, to which the affirmative answer was assumed. I tried saying all sorts of other things like "I was planning on setting fire to the carpet" or "I'm selling my body to local farmers," but she never noticed.

Isobel hardly ever acknowledged my existence. I was too far beneath her. Only worth talking to when there's something to gloat about. So I learned to fend for myself during that summer holiday. I made cheese sandwiches and cooked them in the microwave until the bread went wet and the cheese flowed freely. I had a similar trick for fish finger sandwiches, only with less oozing. Tinned peaches kept me from scurvy and sauces kept me from being too bored to bother eating.

There was nothing for me to do. Nothing. Daytime television does not count as something to do, it is a temporary form of suicide. You can literally feel your own brain cells shutting down in self defence. I tried walking but there was nowhere to go. Up the side of the hill into miles of flat fields of nothing. Down through the steep fields the other way, along the lane to a village with a shop that sold nothing, a pub that would not let me in, old men who stared recreationally and a cricket pitch that no one played cricket on. They just kept the grass really neat. It was like the Earth after a bad movie apocalypse, only without the amusement value of any flesh-eating aliens.

I would have sold my body or my soul for cinema tickets or live music, but no one wanted either and no one offered an escape route. School became a beacon of hope in my future, and that's going some. I didn't even know where I'd be going in the autumn, but even the idea of homework started to look attractive. New people to ignore. The high rates of murders in villages, as portrayed by assorted detective shows started to make sense. I took to drawing up lists of people I could kill and places to hide the bodies. This is probably one of the reasons I now have a therapist.

Eventually, Violent Crispy lured me out for a proper tour. From the way she talked, I knew she'd been rehearsing it. "There used to be a wool mill down in the valley, on the bigger stream, and these were mill worker's cottages. That's why they're so pokey and dark. They were for poor people. Most of my house is new, which is why it's so much nicer, but Mrs Adams didn't even have an indoor toilet when I was a little girl and your grandmother never had a phone or anything. She was really old fashioned. Bit like you, really. You look like her."

"Thanks." I don't look like anyone in my family. I like to pretend that this is because I was hatched out of an egg. I remember my grandmother being like something made out of walnut shells. Looking like her is not a compliment.

"There used to be another house over here, you can see the walls, but there was a murder in it and it got burned down."

"Is it haunted?"

"Kate, it's mostly brambles. Brambles can't be haunted."

"Why not?"

"Because they weren't killed in the brambles, they were killed in the house and not it's not there. Stands to reason."

"They?"

"Whole family."

"Who did it?"

"No one ever found out."

I couldn't tell if she was messing with me, but I'd seen enough Murder She Wrote by then to be very glad of encountering anything a bit more real and plausible. I'm writing the conversations as best I recall them. Some of them are word for word, because I try to remember important things. Some are a best guess, because at the time they didn't seem to matter and I wasn't really paying attention. It's the gist of what I can remember.

My grandmother's house (it didn't feel like my house while I was living there) was at the open end of the valley, angled towards the fields a little bit. Vee's tour took me up the unsurfaced lane between the cottages. I'd thought it was private so hadn't been there. She didn't think it mattered, and I figured I could blame her if there was a problem. The lane turned out longer than I'd thought, the valley too – a deep, steep cleft of a thing, mostly hidden by trees.

"Most of the valley is off limits," Vee said.

I have extra sensory perception tuned to telling when people want you to take their drama seriously. It's probably the only reason I've survived this long. I dutifully took the bait. "Why?"

"It's all fenced off, right through the woods, all the way from here to the top."

Sometimes it's hard to be excited about other people's big revelations. "There must be a gate somewhere," I pointed out.

She smiled triumphantly. "There isn't. I've walked round and round it and there's no way in, unless..." Blatant pause for dramatic effect.

"Unless?"

"There could be a way in from the garden of this last cottage. Wychelm Cottage."

"Sounds a bit spooky." I really was trying my best.

"You wait. There's got to be something hidden in there, don't you think?"

This, apparently, is what living in nowhere land does to a young mind. Dear gods, what must it have been like to grow up here? No wonder my grandmother was barking mad. No wonder my father can't wait to get back to London. No wonder he's such a lunatic.

I know nothing about buildings, but even I could tell this place was old. It looked like it had grown out of the land. There were no straight edges, no right angles. No car and no sign of a drive. No aerial or telephone lines. Heavy curtains in the windows and the kind of plant-covered fence fit for a sleeping princess with a low budget. Even by the eerily quiet valley standards, the place was hushed.

"Rumour has it there's a guy who lives here. I've never seen him, and I've been trying to spy on him for years."

With that, she hooked me. Never mind that I hated her for being pretty and envied her for having halfway decent parents and felt afraid of her because that's mostly how I feel about people. Vee was stalking a mysterious recluse and I wanted in.

I haven't written about the quiet really, have I? Telling the story gets in the way of telling the important things, sometimes. I was expecting the countryside to be quiet compared to London. In some ways it is – very few cars, no sirens, no alarms, no aeroplanes most of the time. I was ready for that. What I hadn't expected was how loud quiet things can be. It's all relative. There's not much background noise, so things stand out more. Cockerels in the morning. I don't mind that. Things in the dark in the trees at night when I'm lying in bed. Rustling things making creepy sounds, sometimes like someone is dying. I don't know what sounds like that. I never asked anyone, I was afraid no one else could hear them or that they meant something I was better off not knowing about.

Wychelm Cottage has another kind of quiet around it. The sort of quiet you get when someone or something is keeping very still and being careful not to make itself obvious. In the daylight, this was okay.

The next day we took packed lunches and went walking. Unzapped cheese for me! Three different kinds of crisps, cola, stale cake. Fending for myself. Life is tough when you can't order takeaway, but at least the adults put edible things in the fridge and freezer with passable frequency. I ate sweet and sour cheese puffs, pot noodles with salad cream, tuna korma over instant mash. A lot of my grandmother's things were still in the kitchen. Nameless and inexplicable, they looked to me like things related to proper cooking. Sometimes, when frying eggs and tinned spaghetti badly in an old pan, I'd got the feeling she was stood behind me, shaking her head in dismay. I did not mix pasta and anti-pasta, just to be on the safe side.

Vee had dainty little sandwiches with lettuce and chicken in them, and nectarines. When she saw my cake and crisps, there was a look, and that look said things about waistlines and skin tones. I'm not the kind of girl you buy fresh fruit for, or make packed lunches for. I get that. I could have done with a friend right then, the sort who has enough shit of their own so they don't want to peer at mine by way of light entertainment.

So we took her beloved daughter picnic and my neglected child picnic and we followed the fence. It was a tall, well secured fence – wire and big wooden posts. There were places holes had been dug to get underneath, but even super-slim Vee would not have got through those. We trudged uphill through dark woodland and I learned things about tree roots and loose rocks and not falling over. We got to the top and had to climb under a barbed wire fence, but that was fairly easy. Then along the edge of a field with an impressive crop of stones growing in it. To our right, trees plunged down into the valley. I could make out my grandmother's house, but the other cottages were hidden by the trees and the shape of the slope. There was no obvious way down.

We stopped in a shady patch and I ate the entirety of the picnic of shame and tried to pretend that it was a totally sensible lunch. After that, Vee lectured me about the importance of fresh fruit for beautiful skin and I wondered if I could somehow force her through the fence and down the steep drop amongst the trees, where hopefully she would be impaled on something and slowly bleed to death. We got all the way round and down and back to Wychelm Cottage and I was forced to admit that no gate existed.

It had not been a wonderful adventure. It had been dull, sweaty and humiliating. I went back to the lonely business of furtively going through my grandmother's things. She hadn't owned much that wasn't useful. Old photos, postcards and paperwork had been stashed in the box-room for later consideration. Which in my family means, "we plan to forget and do nothing." I was hoping for love letters, treasure maps, a gothic diary full of dreadful family secrets. Proof that I'd been stolen at birth, or was the consequence of some dreadful scientific experiment. Anything. I recognised none of the people in the photos, and there were no names.

I don't think I was ever a happy child. In London, I had places to go and people I could be around without much effort and that was okay. I knew other kids and their parents had very different lives to mine. Hell, my own sister had a very different life to mine. That's just how it went. I don't know if it was because of growing up so much in those weeks, or being totally alone so much, but I started to wonder about things that summer – things I'd just taken for granted before. Why was all this happening to me? Was I marked out in some way as different? Was I not thin enough to be worth loving just a little bit? Not clever enough? Not good enough? Who would I have to become to be worth someone's time and bother? Did I want to be like that? Did I have a choice?

I didn't have any answers, and I hated how the questions made me feel. Not being able to figure anything out was horrible. So I started asking other questions instead, after a while. Questions to take my mind off my many woes. What is the opposite of cheese? If you had some anti-matter, where would you put it? What colour is yes? Do the cows know they are cows? Do they know that they are all different cows? Do they care? Looking back, I know I was going a bit mad. Age. Hormones. Lack of cinema.

What I did was totally deliberate, because I needed to think about something other than me. Spending too much time around Vee had me thinking violent violet thoughts. I didn't think what I had in mind could cause any harm. I just took to walking along the fence a lot, and going up the lane to Wychelm

Cottage. I was looking for clues and signs, trying to find out something, anything about the recluse. Not like a TV detective, like a girl who has lost the plot. Looking for a way in.

I started making up little scenarios about meeting him, making friends with him. Old guy? Or young and cute? Mysterious secret, troubled past, hiding from the Mafia, romantically disfigured. Generally misunderstood, but magically making perfect sense to me. I came up with a lot of these, just to pass the time. I persuaded myself that I was in love with him, that we were having a passionate, very secret love affair. I felt drawn, and destined and talked myself into a full blown obsession.

Sometimes, after dark, there were lights behind the curtains. Soft lights, like candles or lamps. I never saw him leave, though. I never caught so much as a glimpse of him.

Early August. Rain. My father had a show in Paris and because of that, he needed to spend time in London first, getting organised. My sister had a chess ballet tournament to be bashed out with tennis rackets whilst dressed for the catwalk. I don't know, nor do I care what she really does. I wasn't paying her any attention. Turns out everyone else was paying even less attention. Afterwards, they all blamed each other loudly for surely having been the one who was supposed to be sorting it all out. They probably blamed me, too, for having caused the whole mess by inconsiderately existing in the first place.

It took me a couple of nights to realise I was the only person in the house and I didn't know when anyone was coming back. I'd seen so little of them, it was only when I ran out of bread that I started to wonder what was going on. I had no money, and I didn't know where they all were. The sensible thing would have been to throw myself on the mercy of the neighbours. No. I just saw it as a perfect opportunity to spend an entire night spying on Wychelm Cottage.

Despite my excitement, I stayed in, and cooked a good meal first. Well, I say cooked. I defrosted a whole box of vol-au-vents, stuffed them with soft cheese from out of a tube, plus fish paste and baked beans, with a tin of cold rice pudding to finish. "It's not my fault I don't know how to cook," I told my grandmother, in case she was listening. "I'm a product of my environment," I said. "Society is to blame." I was giggling by this point, but there had been no alcohol, I swear. I packed snacks, and a bottle of pop, put on my father's raincoat and Isobel's wellies left over from the brief horse period of the previous year. Darkness came, no one returned to stop me. It was fate! I went out into the night, doing my best to be quiet and nonchalant.

All the cottages I could see, aside from my grandmother's were lit up. They looked warm, snug. Families gathered around televisions. Probably no one else here had just eaten cold baked beans out of slightly warm vol-au-vents. I felt radical, but I also felt lonely.

There were no lights on at Wychelm Cottage though. I felt let down. Where did he go at night, round here, without a car? There was a puzzle to work out. Was he sat inside, in the dark, listening to me walking about? That thought made me shiver. I walked up and down a bit, half hoping he'd notice and come out and ask me what I was doing there. It was a scene I had previously rehearsed. That all got dull pretty quickly, so I started poking about in the hedge instead. Some parts of it turned out to be more solid than others. One bit turned out to not be very solid at all, and I pushed my way through, wet leaves slapping my face as I went. For a horrible moment, I thought I was stuck, and then I lurched forward, nearly fell flat on my face, regained my balance somehow. I crept down the side of the cottage. No lights were on at the back, either. Curtains closed. Stillness, like a big animal, waiting. I couldn't see much, even with the torch on. It was an overgrown sort of garden, but there were paths and I followed one, away from the cottage and towards the fenced off, forbidden trees.

At first the trees were occasional, like an old orchard. They looked a bit twisted. Moths flickered around the torch beam. Small things rustled around me, but I kept my nerve. The trees grew thicker, but I could still feel the flagstone path under my feet. I was trespassing, breaking the law, no one else was responsible for me. My life finally felt like my own. I felt real and present, grown up and suddenly very much wiser. Like adulthood had happened to me all at once.

I walked that straight, smooth, flat path for a very long time before I started to think about the geography issues. It seemed like I'd gone too far, given the depth of the cleft. It also seemed far too flat. I stopped and turned to shine the feeble torch back the way I had come. The path disappeared a few feet behind me. Trick of the light, I figured, so I took a few paces back the way I had come, expecting more damp stone flags to come reassuringly into view. They didn't. I turned, and the path ahead looked just the same as it had before. Turned again – only dark soil and trees.

I don't know why it never occurred to me to try and go back the way I'd come even though the path had vanished. I faced the way the path went, and I followed it. That was the moment of crossing over, I feel sure. I don't know where I was when things changed, but that was definitely when. In my choice. I accepted that everything had gone a bit weird and I carried on anyway.

And then, I tell people, I got a bit lost. "For three weeks?" They all ask this. They are, at various times, police persons, social workers, therapists, parents, my new GP, my new new GP, my new therapist and others who do not reveal titles and job descriptions to me. Those folk worry me the most and I tell them as little as I can.

I learned, really quickly, to say what people wanted to hear. I hid. I stole food. I did not want to be found. I was angry with my family and wanted to punish them. I never considered even trying to tell the truth – it was like following the stone path all over again. It seemed obvious which way to go. Truth though, that's complicated. I've told the official story so many times that I almost believe it myself. Except, every night when I dream, I am back on that stone path and heading into the trees and it feels like a part of me is still there.

That first night was not normal night length. I say this with some confidence because I walked all the way through it and I'm not any kind of long distance walker. I did not find the fence, or even the steep side of the valley and I should have done, clearly. Where did I go? I had all sorts of ideas as I was walking about what was going on. Ideas about time and space, half remembered tales about walking back into history, or into a parallel universe, or a secret magic kingdom. Shades of Narnia and The Wizard of Oz. Only I would not be tapping my heels together any time soon to promise 'there's no place like home'. Home wasn't in London anymore and it wasn't my grandmother's house either. It wasn't anywhere. But there were no witches and no munchkins and no oompaloompas and no dinosaurs and no cavemen. Once again, everything I had learned from pop culture turned out to be wrong.

What I did find, was a lovely, tinkling little stream. The path went to it, and stopped about the time it started getting light. I drank the last of the pop and refilled the bottle with water, hoping nothing had died upstream. I remember someone at school telling me you should never drink from mountain streams because there always turns out to be a dead sheep in it, further up. No sign of sheep in ages, and I didn't think there were mountains so hopefully it would be okay.

I considered my options. Downstream ought to mean back towards home. Only there wasn't a stream in our valley, just a muddy trickle. So where did all this water go? Upstream ought to take me through the trees and out onto the top, to the fields of rocks. To where I'd walked with Vee, around the impenetrable fence. Couldn't be that far, I figured. It made sense at the time. Up I went, climbing now, sometimes on rocks, sometimes on narrow paths, following the water. I stopped every now and then to rest and drink. Sometimes I lay down on a flat stone and slept for a while. When I dream about it now, I walk the stone path and I climb and dream that I go to sleep and wake up on the stone path, and climb, and I'm never sure when I've really woken up.

Sometimes I sit in classrooms at school, not able to concentrate and it feels like part of me is there, climbing.

I ran out of food, and I didn't care. There was plenty of water and it tasted reassuring. Did I sleep there and just dream of all that climbing? I don't know. It was a gentle, quiet place. Unthreatening, and a bit unreal. I had no idea where I was trying to get to or how to tell when I got there. I just kept on heading up. All the time it was just me, the tumbling stream, the rocks and the trees. Mostly I couldn't see very far ahead or behind me.

I wasn't angry. I didn't even know before this happened that anger was my default state. It had been, and it is again now, but for a little while there, I found out how it feels not to be growling in rage through every waking hour of the day. No longer feeling like life happened only to other people, not to me. Mostly it was nice. Pretty. I didn't sleep much though and after a couple of nights this had some odd effects on me. My sense of time had been off since I started, but it got even less reliable. Light and dark, long twilights, golden dusks that went on forever. The edges of everything blurred.

Anything seen from the corners of my eyes took on some kind of other life, as though the dreams I'd missed out on were happening anyway. Everything seemed alive, present, animate. It really didn't help that I could no longer tell when I was asleep and when awake. Thinking I was asleep and when I was asleep, dreaming I couldn't sleep, or had gone to sleep.

The more the edges blurred, the more things took on other shapes. Rocks and trees developed eyes and faces. Every stone I climbed over seemed like a person. Some of them would encourage me, others were grumpy or indifferent. The sky became a shifting picture full of sort-of invisible sky beings who I could both see and not see all at the same time. I ate things I thought were cakes, but which did not taste like cake at all. They tasted of mould and old leaves.

I sang a lot and at the time it seemed like I was making up the most amazing, inspired songs anyone had ever sung. Looking back, I have my doubts about that, but I don't remember any of it clearly. I sang to the rock people and the sky people and to the edges of my vision. I sang to the no faces people and the just eyes people and the people who were behind me but always hid when I turned round. I sang to the cakes that were almost certainly not cakes at all, and when I'd eaten them, I sang about them.

I was not quiet, or subtle. I was not hiding. You'd think, if anyone had been looking for me at all in that tiny valley during the three weeks I was missing, that they could hardly fail to notice me. And yet, I was unfound.

I did try and talk to all this about one of the therapists – not about what happened, but more the feeling of it. The gentleness, the possibility and the not being angry.

"Why do you think you can't feel that way the rest of the time?" she asked.

"Did I mention my family to you at all?" I came back - I'd talked about them a lot, obviously.

"You're very hostile towards them," she observed. Then I got a lecture about how fortunate I was – it wasn't like I'd been beaten or starved or sexually assaulted, after all. I had a lot to be grateful for. I needed to learn how to practice gratitude. Basically she had me down as a spoiled brat. Me! Isobel's the spoilt, precious one. I'm just a bit part in the great family drama. But she couldn't see past the money – my father's money. He was paying her to make me be quiet, is what it came down to. He wasn't paying her to take my side or even to give a shit about me, just to reassure social services that everything was in hand. So I don't talk to therapists. I don't talk to anyone, much. At first, when we came back to London, I wasn't even allowed to go out on my own. Permanently grounded, or on a leash. Hideous. Forced to tag along to Isobel's football training. What happened to tennis? Isobel's auditions. She never got picked for anything and that was my one consolation.

Sometimes, I wonder why I came back. I could have stayed there. No one would have found me. In the end I'd probably have starved to death, but that's fine. I think about dying a lot because my life is never going to be any good and no one will ever take me seriously or actually want me. I am just an unwelcome burden on my family, not good enough for them. They would probably be a lot happier if I'd never come back. I'd be happier. I think about jumping under buses, but worry about getting the timing wrong and getting horribly injured and having to live with it. I'd be even more of a joke then – the girl so thick and useless that she couldn't even manage to top herself. That would be even worse than how things are now.

Tube. High building. Overdose. Slit wrists. No matter which method you think about, there's so much scope to mess it up if you don't know how to do it properly, and there's no way to practice. Why doesn't someone run classes? How to top yourself cleanly and efficiently in ten easy steps. People jump in front of tube trains all the time. I reckon a course on doing it would make a fortune.

When an animal is deemed useless, it is shot or put to sleep. We're doing Hitler at school. He was into all this sort of thing. I'm not so sure it's a bad idea – not if it's voluntary. Lots of people would say yes to a quick, tidy sort of death. Of course Hitler didn't ask for volunteers. More of an issue if you didn't agree to it, but it's still just checking out early. No one gets out of here alive. That's some sort of consolation.

My GP refuses to put me on antidepressants because of my age and tells me if I could just stop thinking morbid thought I'd be fine. He's so helpful. I'm sure it's also true that if I could just stop being useless, I'd be fine. Stop being thick. Grow some talent. Get a fairy godmother to lift the curse I am clearly under and turn me into the kind of duck all the other ducks are cool with. What am I waiting for?

I left because of the rain. It started lightly enough, no big deal in my father's raincoat. I kept walking to keep warm, and I think at that point I didn't really know how to stop anymore anyway. As I went, the raindrops got bigger, and wetter. My jeans soaked through and carried water down into my wellies until I was squelching with every step. In the end even the coat started to give up around the shoulders and the water got in to every part of me. There's waterproof, and then there's biblical flood proof, and this coat was not that thing. With the wet came the cold, seeping right into my bones in a way I'd not believed happened to people outside of books we read at school. Even that didn't make me turn back, but in the end, the water became too much.

The stream became a torrent, spilling out onto the rocks and paths beside it, pushing me away. Slippery stone plus knackered wellies doesn't make for good walking. The water backed me into the woods, which by that point were about as steep as they should have been all along. I felt like everything was telling me to leave – the rocks and the rain, and the trees – it felt like a clear message.

Last year's leaves on the ground. Wet. I learned a thing. I learned that wet holly leaves on a wet, steep hill when it's wet underfoot and you have wet shoes on, means falling over. Pretty much straight away. Down I went. Then I learned that a wet raincoat and wet jeans don't help much when you're trying not to slide down a slippery bank. I couldn't get back on my feet.

No matter what I tried, it soon became clear that down was my only option. I could stop for short periods by hanging on to tree trunks. Wet hands plus wet tree trunks plus cold doesn't work for long. I skidded, tried to avoid the worst of the thorn patches, the rocks, the low branches, but every few yards gave me another bruise or cut. There were a lot of yards.

I felt certain the valley itself was throwing me out. Trees, earth and water seemed to be working together to remove me. I wondered if I'd done something wrong, or if my time was up. I didn't really fight to stay, I could have tried harder rather than just going with it. Maybe it was a test, and if it was, then I think I failed. I keep thinking about it and wondering if I could have done differently, and never come back here at all. I wish I had never come back.

For most of the journey down, all I could think about was how to stop falling and hurting. I ran out of down, eventually, and just lay where I'd landed, wondering where that was, and what would happen next if I did nothing. Then I spotted the light. The day was gloomy at this point, not proper dark, but enough to show that not far away from me, something glowed. At the time it looked like the kindest, prettiest thing I had ever seen. For almost all of the time I'd been out on my own, the only light had been in the sky – my torch having died early on. I'd got used to natural light, and no light. That nearby glow spoke to me of warmth, shelter, food and all the things I'd survived without. I wanted to go home. I had no sense of having a home anywhere in the world, but all the same, I wanted to go there. I headed towards the light.

What came next happened very quickly. So fast that at the time I didn't know what to make of it, and just let it all happen. There are clear images in my head, and they're like photographs for the most part. Still and vivid and not moving into each other very well. I'm not going to write it like it probably happened. I'm going to write what I remember, what I felt. These minutes were some of the biggest ones in my whole life.

Picture one: I can't see where the light is coming from exactly, but I see the stone walls of a building. Flagstones. Plants with shiny leaves. It's wet here, too. Everything gleams and looks unreal, as though I'm seeing a flat scene painted on glass.

Picture two: This is the most important picture. When I see it I know I've been waiting my whole life for this moment. The light comes from a lamp, and above the lamp is a face. A sad face. Male, old, beardy. His face is round, and looks like it was made for smiling, but right now he is so desperately sad, and sorry, and I want to ask what's wrong but there's no chance for me to do that. I can't tell what colour his eyes are.

He isn't tall, or pretty. Not in the least bit like anyone I have ever fancied. He's broad and solid, a big coat round his shoulders, strong looking hands holding the lantern. I want to step inside this moment and keeping looking into his face. I don't know what I'm feeling, what it should be called but it is big and heavy, as though a giant boulder has just rolled right over me and I'm stood there in shock with no words and no idea what to do.

Picture three: This one comes with a barrage of noise, flashing lights, bright yellow jackets, hands on my arms, questions. Not quite a still image this time, more like a photograph taken inside a whirlwind and badly animated. Everything is too loud, too colourful, spinning around me. I want to go back into the dark and the quiet, but they do not let me. Only in this picture do I know why, or at least some part of why the man with the lantern looks so sad: he can't stop them. He can't save me from what is happening, and if he could have done, he would. He feels badly because he can't help me. This, and only this, I am totally sure of.

Who was he? Did I imagine him? Given the 'gone for three weeks' issue, clearly what I remember of these events isn't totally trustworthy. But of all the things from that time, the memory of his face is the most real thing. Does that mean something?

Then it all kicked off, of course. Police. Questions. Ambulance. Embarrassing medical check-up. More questions. A drip, which I kept telling them I didn't need and they kept telling me I had to have. Once they were sure my body was okay, they all started in earnest on my head, and they've never really stopped with that, and it's been months now.

Of course what I got in private from my parents was mostly blame. Loud and shouty blame from my mother. Quiet disappointment blame from my father. Isobel did a nice sideline in how dare you be the centre of attention blame. Well, that was me cured. She can have all my share of the limelight forever. People paying attention means no privacy. Not even inside my own head. It means people feeling entitled to read your notebooks and there being meetings where adults discuss you but no one tells you what anyone said or decided. I have a lot to be angry about.

At night I dream I am still climbing the path beside the stream and going ever deeper into the woods. So deep they will never find me. Not even a flood is going to wash me out now. When I'm dreaming, I know that I never really left there. All this mess with coming back to London and being constantly assessed is just an illusion. The valley is real, and I am still walking. When I'm awake, I'm less sure about it. The world around me seems plenty real enough, and I dream of getting out. I don't know where to go, though. The sea? The circus? Who would accept me? Where do I belong? I don't know. Not here, any more. Last year I would have said London was home, but I've come back different and with no words to explain that change to myself, or anyone else.

I feel like my life, my whole self is on hold now, but I don't know what I'm waiting for. I'm trying to pass myself off as a normal person, but I feel like a fake all the time. No one understands, and I don't dare try and explain. No one here can give me answers. Maybe the hermit guy from Wychelm

Cottage knows. I keep wondering if it was him I saw that night. He had the kind of face you could tell secrets to. I can't begin to imagine what he would say to me, or what his voice would sound like.

I keep falling back into that moment. His face. Lamplight on rain-slick flagstones. So much mystery in his face. More than who he is – in the usual sense of putting names to faces. Who is he? Why is he sad, and sorry for me? What does he know that I do not? He looks at me like he cares about me. Not like I'm annoying him, or not good enough, but as though it is my hurt that is making him feel sad. My going. My past or my future or maybe all of these things. It is a very big deal to have someone look at you like they really care. Especially when it makes you realise that this has never happened to you before. Not to you, of course, whoever you are, my hypothetical diary-reading intruder. To me. I still find it hard to own that. Me. Cared about, and not cared about.

If I could step back into that image, what would I do? Put my hand on his arm, to know that he was properly real and to see if he'd be okay with me doing that. Generally I do not touch people, but I would make an exception for him. I would tell him my name, and apologise for being in his garden, and his valley. I guess they must both be his. I can see why the big fence now. The not-subtle hint to stay out. But, even so, I don't think he was angry with me for sneaking in.

"I'm Kate, sorry about the trespassing, but your valley is really amazing." It's as well I said nothing. Everything I could say sounds stupid. Everything I want to say sounds small and ordinary and unworthy of what happened to me.

My parents tell me we are never, ever going back there. They are selling the house. "If you try and go back there," Isobel told me yesterday – clearly enjoying herself – "If anyone there sees you, they will call the police."

"I'm hardly going to prison," I said.

"Oh no," Isobel came back. "Mum says they will lock you up in a place for mental people, pump you full of drugs to make sure you can't do anything, and that will be you sorted out for the rest of your life."

"She never said that." A feeble reaction on my part. It is so easy to imagine her saying exactly that.

"I'd visit you," Isobel said.

"Clearly, that will help."

"No, not to help. To gloat."

We are to remember that I am a spoiled brat who has nothing to complain about and should be grateful for all the good things in her life. "A diary will help you get some perspective, Katy. It will help you see that really things aren't that bad and will show you your negative thoughts in their true light."

I want to strangle that fucking overpaid shit of a therapist. Is that negative enough for you yet?

My Second Life: 21

3rd September.

Guy downstairs howling again last night. Played Oasis very loudly until three am. How can anyone pretend to be a werewolf while listening to Oasis? Entirely wrong. In other news, I have bought a hat and now I have no money until Wednesday. Emma says I must now sell my body for food. She says I should have bought thigh boots instead as these would have helped with the sex trade project and the hat does not. I could busk. If I sing on street corners, people would pay me to shut up and go away. Like a protection racket, only with more bum notes and the violent slaughter of classic rock ballads.

7th September.

I hate marmite. I hate toast. I hate the man downstairs and I hate every single song in his music collection. I hate my job. I hate the electricity bill. I hate that it is autumn. I hate that I am doing nothing and have nothing to say and almost no one to say it to. I hate pigeons.

8th September.

Solicitors letter from Whappit, Whappit and Smerge. Too afraid to open it. Afraid it is another bill. Cease and desist? What have I done? Who have I offended? If I ignore it, will that make it worse? Can I pretend it never showed up? Is it some debt I've forgotten about? No money, nothing doing. Will send toast as payment. No marmite left.

9th September.

My mother's uncle went a bit mad once because he tried to live on a diet of very small tins of fish and cup-a-soup. It may be happening to me, too. I keep dreaming about bacon. Money tomorrow. Proper food. Virtue food with fruit in it. No impulse hat buying. I've got fourteen hats now. How many hats does a person need? I think the toast is messing with my head. Nearly there. What is it with my family and food?

10th September.

Saw the man from downstairs. Clearly I am still mad from the poor diet because I thought he looked fit. Even knowing about the howling and the horrors of his music collection. Hairy guy. Shaggy. Definitely could be a werewolf.

12th September.

Em found the Whappit letter. Apparently she was tidying the airing cupboard. Emma's madness is hard to predict because it manifests in such subtle, mundane ways. Who in their right mind tidies an airing cupboard? She opened the letter and read it, and then she made me read it. Said letter was weird with no content, just asking me to come to their office, which is in Gloucestershire, of all places. Sounded like it was written about a hundred years ago. For a joke. By someone with no sense of humour. How many days of food budget will a train fare cost? Could be a scam, seems like a waste of money, but I'm curious.

13th September.

I dream about the hills again. I'm walking the footpath, the one everyone walks and in the distance I can see a big, green hill, the one on its own. In the dream I remember being there and that it is an amazing place, and I miss it, but now I'm awake I have no idea where it is or how to get to it, or even if I've ever really been there. I've got a memory of being on that hill and feeling wonder, but I don't know if I'm just remembering another dream. In my dream dictionary, hills = life challenges and walking = progress towards success. I feel let down by this.

16th September.

If I write all of this very slowly then perhaps by the time I've got to the end of it, it will magically have turned into something I can get my head round and be ok with. Right now I feel like I might explode, and this, in traditional family style is totally my grandmother's fault. So I went by trains, all the way. Plus some walking at the end to find the crumbling building that is home to the offices of Whappit, Whappit and Smerge. Or 'Shelob's Lair' as I am inclined to call it for the sheer number of alarmingly big spiders in there. As well Em did not come with me as she may have died from fear.

I've not said any of this out loud yet. It does not seem real. It's like the nanosecond in a dream when you know that the sea is going to turn out to be a pie, or that time has reversed, or there is uncanny magic flowing towards your fingertips. This is a reality deal-breaker. If I say it out loud, anything could happen. Gravity might stop working.

I own a house. A whole one. Outright. I, who have no money for food this week, own a house. And possibly I do have some money, but they aren't sure how much. In her will, my grandmother left her entire estate to me, to be kept in trust until I reached the age of 21, which I have duly done. Here I am. Here it is. Why just me? Why not my father? Or a three way split with my sister in it too? Apparently he tried to contest it, and failed.

They never told me. I inherited the house, and they never told me. I lived in that house for a while and did not know it was even mine. Why? But then, when did they ever tell me anything if they could avoid it? My solicitors – no really – my solicitors who have already been paid by my grandmother's estate, will look into what's been done with the house. It hasn't been sold, it should therefore have been rented out to earn a nice pot of money for me. My guess is that it will be damp and empty with things in the fridge from when we were there seven years ago.

I hate my parents, but in a calm way. Not in a going round to their respective homes and killing them sort of way.

There was a letter from my grandmother, to Miss Kathleen Sylvia West, because she felt sure I had too much sense to have got married by the age of twenty one! She said, "I know how life is going to be for you. This will rebalance things and you have a good heart. Take care of the land and do not sell the house to some city idiot." My father of course being a lad of the soil who had chosen the city, and my mother is city idiot personified. I wish I'd known my grandmother better. Apparently I had an ally there. A friend. My whole childhood would have been totally different if I'd known that. I wonder if Isobel knew about any of this? Perhaps that's why she hated me. She couldn't stand to be anything other than the favourite.

I have told Em. I have made the crazy words come out of my face. She proposed marriage – she would very much like to marry my country pad regardless of the state it may be in. I have promised to consider her as a possible concubine and she bought me chips as an investment in this arrangement.

17th September.

Shoved rude note under door of man downstairs. Cannot take any more Oasis.

18th September.

Brief visit from the police, who, like my neighbour downstairs had taken the line 'I will take your champaign supernova and shove it up your arse' as a more literal threat than I had intended. Mid conversation with them, and entirely audible set of lyrics came up through the floor, rattling everything, especially me. One of the cops said "Gallagher's a wanker anyway," and they went downstairs for a little chat about noise pollution instead. There are laws about that! Result!

19th September.

Dreamed about a house, and on every floor the corridors got narrower and the stairwell too, and the stairs got steeper until I was climbing ladders up chutes that I could barely squeeze my shoulders into. I don't know why I never went in any of the rooms. Dream dictionary says ladders = progress in your career. House = your inner self. Nothing on not opening doors. Getting narrower is about the desire for weight loss, which is also all about unlocking your inner potential to find your success. So that's all clear now. Umm.

20th September.

Dreamed about an angry cabbage and that I had to row it in a boat across a big, misty lake and all the time the cabbage was shouting abuse at me in Liam Gallagher's voice and telling me things that made no sense at all about how I was just a loaf full of blood. I blame the toast. Dream dictionary says cabbage = healthy living and good lifestyle choices. Misty = lack of clarity about your future career path. Lake = opportunity for transformation. Rowing = making progress in your life. Why is everything about making progress in my life? Anyone not dead is moving forwards in some way, it's the most empty, banal shite imaginable. If there is any direction available aside from forwards, I have yet to discover it.

21st September.

Caught myself humming Oasis tunes. I feel dirty and wrong. In other news, my boss is a dick, and it's getting really hard not to point this out to him. Apparently the last 'girl' who complained about sexual harassment lost her job, and I should be glad he's only pinching my bottom.

22nd September.

I hate my job. There has to be something better than this. It can't all be this bad. Started job hunting again, but everything asks for qualifications I don't have, or a car, or experience I haven't got, or a heady mix of those things. Feel useless.

Em came home with a copy of Bridget Jones's Diary to cheer me up. Now feel less useless. Feel V. Smug and on top of life because apparently there are more things to be neurotic about then I'd ever considered before. Hat addiction comparatively v. good. Pigeons v. bad. Re-read my own diary entries in light of this very popular book and wondered about publishing deals. "V. small book" Em said. Now officially done that joke to death and will never speak of it again.

25th September.

Wondering how long it takes for a Whappit to do all the incomprehensible legal things that have to be done and when I might find out if there is any money for me. If I write that I keep thinking up convoluted ways to kill my boss so it looks like an accident, this may help me not to do it because the police would take my diary as evidence and I would be thwarted. Pushing him down the stairs is my number one preference. Slowly add arsenic to his afternoon cake, having somehow extracted arsenic from apple pips. I have to get out of this job, I cannot take any more of his gross innuendoes.

26th September.

I dreamed that all the members of Oasis were trying to kill me, only I don't really know what they look like so they were all blank faces with anoraks and hoods, and there were a dozen of them, and they were all armed with kitchen implements. I'd never thought blenders were sinister before. Dream dictionary had nothing on Oasis aside from the haven in a desert which = omen of career success. No anoraks, nothing on people with no faces, no blenders. Kitchen = nourishment, comfort and reassurance, which is an unlikely interpretation for a nightmare. I consoled myself by buying a new hat. Well, new to me. Em says I am allowed a hat habit if I can be either cheap or occasional about it.

27th September.

Isobel phoned at three am because she was feeling awful and needed to talk. I kept her talking long enough to be sure that she wasn't actually trying to kill herself this time. Which is funny, because by that point I would cheerfully have done it for her. She kept saying things like 'I just don't see any point in my life'. I was really good, I did not agree with her once. I am a saint. She only gets her picture in glossy magazines when falling drunken and underclad out of nightclubs in the wake of proper celebrities. None of these people are her friends, and she never gets her name mentioned, not even when you can see her tits. It's not much of a career, really. As Z list celebrities go, she's still a wannabe. I may not have much, but I have some dignity. And I have a house. Still feels weird.

28th September.

Seventeen page handwritten letter from my mother. Eighty two percent unreadable, which given the readable eighteen percent may be a blessing. Part of me sometimes wishes she'd phone, or visit me and then I get letters like this and I remember why it is better to get letters and not to see her at all. It started "I have had a letter from your solicitors" and that was really the only nice bit. All my fault. All my father's fault and my grandmother's fault and so unjust to poor Isobel who was always a much nicer child then me anyway. Such a waste, leaving a house to me. Long justifications for what she did and did not do – I think. I feel like the inside of me fell down a long flight of stairs and is covered in bruises. I guess at least now I have an answer to why she always seemed to have such a massive problem with me. I was given something she wanted. Something worth money.

Had a row with Em. Horrible. My bruises now have bruises on them. She says I shouldn't take it so personally – fine for her to say. Her parents are nice. No one ever forgot her or told her she was a useless waste of space and time. She doesn't understand and I got cross with her because I wanted her to understand how much I was hurting and now I feel even worse. Maybe it is me. Maybe it always was. Maybe most of my family hate me because that's all I deserve.

29th September.

In the dream I am back at my grandmother's house. There are more doors than I remember. It's definitely her house, and not mine, and I know this is important. There is something here I have to do, and I don't know what it is, so I wander around the place trying to remember what should be outside the windows. In the dream, the windows are blank, and I know that the outside will only come back if I can remember it properly, but I'm stuck. Dream Dictionary says doors = opportunity. Windows = clarity or a new perspective. I put the dream dictionary in the sink and set fire to it. I feel lighter, cleaner and more at peace with the world for having done that. At same time, tested smoke alarm which it turns out is broken. I feel strangely virtuous.

3rd October.

Letter from my solicitors, including a message from my father, who, for fuck's sake, can't manage a seventeen page rant and has to talk to me via someone else. Fuck them. Fuck them all. There is no money from the house. It has not been rented out, it has been left empty. It could have squatters in it. It could be derelict. They were entrusted with looking after it for me and they just didn't bother. At least my father has the decency not to fob me off with wet excuses. Mother guilty conscience any? Father's guilty conscience is to be cleansed with a bloody great cheque. It feels like I am being bought off. Paid to shut up and go away and not make any trouble or cause embarrassment. Fine. I'll take the money. I can't imagine speaking to either of them now. What is there to say? Dear parents, thank you for treating my whole life with total contempt. As you have now given me some money, I guess you think everything has been tided up.

I have to decide whether it's worth using the money to fix the house to sell, or rent, or to keep the lump sum and sell the house as it is, or something else. My Gran did not want me to sell it and I feel some loyalty to her. I don't know what to do. A more adulty adult is needed here.

4th October.

Shit day at work. Worse for all hopes of a rapid escape being lost. Isobel phoned this evening. Why has Dad given me all this money? It's not fair. She can't get him to give her any more money. Is it true about the house? What have I done to make mum so unhappy? Why won't anyone tell her what is going on? I hung up on her. I've never done that before. It felt really good.

7th October.

Back in my grandmother's house. Mostly as before – too many doors and nothing outside the windows. My grandmother present. Only I don't really know what she looked like and I'm guessing that's why she had all these different faces in the dream. I don't know who she was. She kept saying "I wouldn't do it like that," and "This really isn't helping." She sounded like my mother. I don't know what a benevolent grandmother is supposed to sound like. I've been thinking about that all day. More like afternoon tea with cream and jam on scones! Like a fire in the grate. Patient. I don't know if I'm remembering or imagining. I have to go back to the house. I have some camping gear. If it's awful there I can stay in the garden while I figure things out.

11th October.

The house is awful. Damp, dust, mould. Mice – some of whom are very dry and very dead. Spiders who, given their size, may have been living on a diet of mice. Garden a jungle. I opened all the windows and made a token gesture at cleaning. Pointless. Half afraid that if I clean too much, there will be nothing left at all. The whole place is just dust and memories staying house-shaped out of habit. I feel like I'm a me of many years ago. Abandoned. I haven't changed at all. And I am also someone else entirely. Both are true. I have to keep looking out of the windows to make sure it is all still there. Now I know what it's supposed to look like outside, I feel safer.

12th October.

Didn't really sleep. Half awake dreams – of spiders, mice, not sure what was real. Camped on the floor downstairs. Seemed safest. Moonlight through rotten curtains. Muzzy head today. Supposed to walk to the next town to get the one bus to the nearest station to get back to London. Flat. Em. Job. I don't know what to do about this house. I am so tired of everything and I don't know what to do. What happens if I do nothing?

13th October.

Walked to the nearest village, small shop, London prices. Beans on toast. I am still here. I should not be here. I should be at work. He'll fire me. Half the time I feel like a useless, crazy fraud of a person. Em will be worried. There is no phone here. Have water and electric – father not a total failure. Have beans and no job. It's so quiet here. I want to sleep forever. Let the house fall down around me and the brambles grow over me and never have to think about anything ever again.

14th October.

I need a structural survey, because the house is so old and has been empty for so long. I could stay here, clean, redecorate, sort out. I will need a bicycle. Then rent it out, move out, do something else. Change direction. I could be a bit in control of my life, not just floating from one thing to another, one week to another. Tried to call Em from the phone in the village. No answer. Got to write to her and tell her I'm not coming back. None of my stuff is worth fetching. Clean slate. New life. I hope she'll forgive me.

18th October.

Tidy. Clean. Eat. Sleep. Walk to village shop. Fantasise about bicycles. Check outside of windows is still outside of windows. Not much to write about in terms of what I'm doing. Giant spider novelty has worn off. Can't map what I remember from before onto this place at all. So much has changed in the valley, or my memory is wonky, or both. Probably both.

I remember getting lost for a few days. God only knows how. The valley just doesn't seem to be big enough to get that lost in. But then, I wasn't the sharpest pencil in the box as a teen. Still not the sharpest! Now at least have the sense not to go ambling about in unfamiliar woods in the dark.

I've been up the lane a few times now, to the cottage that has the only access to the woods. It all looks very quiet. Very ordinary. What did I expect? Mr Tumnus maybe, or a side door into Diagon Alley. This, as Em could probably tell me, is a consequence of my never reading any proper, grown-up books. Sometimes I miss Em. Mostly I don't, perhaps that makes me a bit of a heartless bastard, but there we are. Right now she seems a long way away and a long time ago. This nameless corner of the map is rather dark and feels lonely. I think some of the other cottages must be holiday homes. Most of the time I feel like there's no one else for miles. I feel very small. This place, this corner doesn't have a name. We're just numbers on Field Road, Cotscombe, and Cotscombe the village is itself is miles away. This isn't a place, it's a something else.

19th October.

Walked up to the cottage again today. The one at the neck of the valley. The tight bit. Is there a proper term for this? Neck? Sphincter? Don't know. Saw a figure at the window, perhaps watching me. Felt a bit creepy. Then I realised I am the one doing the weird stalker stuff, this is just someone who lives here. I remember the games I used to play, and the daydreaming about the recluse back in that long, strange summer. In love with the idea of outsiders and eccentrics. Waiting to be seen, wanting to be recognised and known. To find a place I belonged and people who would see some merit in me. I was such an optimist.

21st October.

Em sent one of my hats to me in the post. No note, just one lonely hat. It made me cry. It seems very symbolic but I don't know what she wants me to think.

22nd October.

I did a lot of complicated things with buses, got lost twice, but am now the happy owner of a mountain bike and the world is my oyster. Probably in the sense of being a bit damp and smelling of fish. I bought some tools and some DIY books, I've got mail order catalogues and I'm not afraid to use them! Slightly afraid I'll have no idea what to do with anything I order. I've always wanted to be practical. It seems like a good time to learn.

24th October.

There's a footpath, comes down the side of the wooded valley, right along the edge of the garden for Wychelm Cottage. The leaves are mostly down so I could see in through the hedge. Nothing much to look at in the garden, all very ordinary – veg plot, compost heap, fruit trees. I don't know what I was looking for, but I can't see it. I keep going back, looking for answers to questions I've not really figured out how to ask yet. Not finding any helpful insights, unshockingly. I've dreamed so many times about what happened here when I was a kid. It's hard to keep the memories straight – they get jumbled up with the dreams. It's a compulsion, coming here. I can't explain it properly – okay I can create explanations but they are really just excuses, not truth. I'm like someone returning to the scene of their crime. It's like my bones need to be on this particular bit of soil. There's something a bit morbid about it.

No eureka moments. No loose floorboard hiding evidence of ancient mysteries or family shame. No strange artefacts hidden up the chimney. I've looked for those, repeatedly, they aren't here. No wild flashes of insight. Just this urge to stay put.

25th October.

So there I was, peering through the hedge again today when all of a sudden there was a face on the other side, peering back. Nearly wet myself. "Were you trying to look at my moist cleft again?" he asked. I think I blushed with all of my skin. I also lost my balance and fell on my arse in the leaf-litter, which does not aid a person's self esteem muchly. He laughed at me, but not in an especially mean way. Not unkindly sounding. "You are allowed to knock on the door," he said. "If you want to stick your nose in the cleft." What to say? I couldn't think of anything clever. He seems funny, rude, unnerving... I'm totally out of my depth.

26th October.

I took biscuits as bribe, talisman and weapon of preference. Knocked on the door. He is the same guy from seven years ago. He's got really distinctive eyes. An unusual shade of blue. I can see his face clearly in my mind, but I can't work out how to describe it. Nose, mouth, symmetry etc. What makes that distinctive? Not a young face, but not old, either. Smile lines, frown creases. Never still. Fierce, playful, dangerous, reassuring. I don't know. How do you read a face? How to see the person in the skin? He laughed a lot, mostly at me. Told me I was the best looking thing he had seen in a long time. Everyone else round here is over sixty, and I pointed that out, and he laughed.

From his garden, the 'moist cleft' looks even smaller. Tea, biscuits, weather, birds, innuendoes. "I knew you'd come back," he said, when I was leaving.

"You invited me to stick my noise in your cleft, how could I refuse?"

"I didn't mean today, although that's an open offer. I meant here. I knew you'd come back here."

So I guess he does remember me from last time. Not sure how I feel about any of this.

29th October.

I had a dream in which my grandmother was sat in the garden with me, here. It was summer and we were drinking tea out of turtle shells and the teapot was a little house on chicken legs that kept wandering around the table. "He's a bit of a man-slut really, but he can't help his own nature," my grandmother said, as though this were the kind of thing grandmothers say all the time. "Try to own him and he'll buck you off." The teapot laid an egg, and inside the egg was this house and the land around it, and I could see that we were in the garden, drinking tea.

31st October.

I have a lot of candles lit. It feels like something ought to happen tonight. It is appropriately dark and chilly, and quiet. Nothing is going to happen unless I make it happen. So maybe I should do that. Go out. Do something.

I'm not sure what day it is. It ought to be the first of November, but I have a feeling it isn't. I remember how the time went before and I need to try and catch some of the memory of this before it slips through my fingers. Even as I try to remember it, I feel the details are slipping away, and all I can make words do is catch the tail of a shadow.

I could remember so clearly everything that happened before. I knew exactly where the weak point in the hedge would be and that I could climb through. I wasn't afraid of being caught. Half wanted to be found. His garden was full of moonlight. Evan's garden. I don't remember when he told me his name.

Everything there was silvered and unearthly, like the regular world, familiar but also otherly, as though everything had fallen under a moon spell. Not a sound. Not a breath of wind.

I heard him come out of the cottage, humming to himself. Like he didn't know I was there. At first I thought of running, but I didn't have to run from him, he wasn't hunting me. I heard his humming voice float down the path, and I followed after him instead. He must have known I was there all along, but he said nothing, showed no sign of knowing. He sped up, I kept up. He ran, and I followed. A tag game. A chase game. Fox and hounds like we played at school, only me being the only hound and he my quarry. Hunted him through the dark garden, smells of soil and old fallen leaves, soft autumn decay and fermenting fruit. Couldn't see him, couldn't see the ground but it didn't slow me. I can't explain what I was doing, not properly. My blood was singing. Following his scent and the feel of his footsteps on the soil. Heat pounding blood rushing chase with the night in my brain and no idea what I'd do if I caught him. A game with its own rules, that I'd find out by playing. A game that played us, for its own purposes. Did he know what we were doing? Impossible to say. Maybe this is his sport and he's played at it many times before.

I've walked that garden in daylight, I know how big it is. How far did we run? And where? Into the neverland of my faulty memory. Into the night at the end of my childhood. I couldn't bring him down unless he chose to let me. It seemed, in the darkness, that other things ran invisibly with us. Not fears. Nothing so simple.

I wanted to bite and tear, taste blood, sweat, flesh. I do not know who I was. This is not me. This is not how I feel. I wanted to hunt him down, subdue and possess. My grandmother's voice in my head, cautioning against ownership. A spell broken. I stopped running. Heart slowing, breath quietening. Just the cool of a moonlit night, and trees, and a fading hunger that left a bitter taste in my mouth. I've never been so lost. Not a geographical issue, but a sense of my everyday self torn away, leaving nothing I recognise. A vicious animal impulse without the justification of being a hungry predator.

I walked back slowly. My head not knowing the way home and hoping my feet had a better idea. Not really able to see much – the moon making a mad half-world of untrustworthy shapes. I didn't hear him catch me up, just felt a hand on my arm in the darkness.

"Interesting choice," he said.

I didn't ask what he meant – I regret that now. I just hoped he knew the way back. I wondered where the other choices led. The choice not to be out here in the first place. The choice to run away. The choice to keep hunting. Game over, not knowing if I'd won or lost, or what was at stake. Not knowing what he wanted of me, or what I wanted from him. Not having the words to ask.

The garden opened up before us. "What if I told you this was Eden?" he asked.

"Liar, poet or madman," I guessed.

He picked an apple and offered it to me. "Fruit from the tree of the knowledge of good and evil," he said.

I took it, took a bite without hesitating. A sharp apple, crisp and fresh. "What do I know?" I asked him.

He came back with, "Less all the time."

Good-oh.

3rd November.

So there's a missing day somewhere. Just the one. It's as well I have the radio to check. Actually two missing days because I have no idea where today went or what I did with it. I feel like I ought to go and talk to Evan about what happened. But at the same time it's like when you have a one night stand with someone and it all goes weird and even seeing them in the distance feels awkward. Because of the projectile vomiting, or the honking noises, or the picture of William Shatner over their bed or whatever it was this time. It occurs to me that I may have had more than my fair share of awkward one night stands. Not all of it was my fault. It's not like I kissed him. He hasn't seen my bum. I didn't catch him weeing into a fish tank. In the grand scheme of things, it should be fine. But I can't quite face going up there and I don't know what to say to him. I'm scared. If I ask "what is it with your garden anyway" and the answer is dull, that would be depressing. Like he put LSD in my tea. The alternatives are that I've gone quite mad, or through the looking glass. Is that preferable?

4th November.

Dreamed that Em posted all of my hats back, individually, only each hat was a bit of my life and they were all singing. All different songs. Except the last hat, which sang Oasis songs until all the other hats went quiet. Woke up feeling like all the things I hated about my old life weren't so terrible after all. And all my other old lives and old versions of me are on my mind now and I wonder if running away is just part of who I am.

8th November.

Big serious grownup day. There are things that need doing on the house – like the wiring – where I just don't have the skills and could die horribly if I try and fail. Can't really afford to get someone in who knows what they're doing. Can borrow against the value of the house. Nervous about debt. Then what? Do not want to turn into Isobel, depending on the paternal guilty conscience for handouts. No work anywhere round here unless I want to try becoming a B&B. Sounds horrible. People and mornings do not mix. I have been liking not living with people, not hearing people making little people noises on the other sides of walls at all hours of the day and night. Quiet is the best friend I ever had. There's a thing to know. Rent the house out? Income stream could cover debt and then some. But in that case, where do I live? What to do? Beyond survival, I don't really know what I want.

9th November.

Cycled to town to see bank people. Solicitors, letting agents. I said as a joke 'so do you have any other ruins I could live in?' They're also an estate agent. Turns out they do have a whole host of abandoned, empty, falling down places with and without roofs, planning permission, interior plumbing, road access... the buildings that missed the memo about the twentieth century. There are, it turns out, people who live by buying old wrecks, inhabiting them while doing them up and then selling them on and starting again. It's got a definite appeal. Gran's place is worth enough to borrow what I need, and have the rents cover the loan plus a little bit over. I haven't burned through Dad's money yet. It's not going to be easy, but it is possible. I'd be living by my skills, such as they are. Never again the creepy pervert boss! It just seems such an amazing idea that I could be good at this. I could be good at something. I wish I had someone who would be excited for me right now.

12th November.

Impulse-bought a ruin in an auction based on the bank saying I could possibly have the loan. Paperwork madness begins! Which seems to mean lots of long distance cycle trips in the cold November rain and turning up soaked and smelling inexplicably like a wet dog to places where I then have to try to convince people in suits that I am some sort of responsible adult. More cycling awaits, at the end of which, I will either be superfit, or dead. Possibly both. I'll be the zombie lurching forward shouting 'drains' and 'must get planning permission'. It I put my tent in the kitchen and buy some really sturdy water and mouse proof boxes, throw the last of my money at getting the roof fixed, eat only beans and rice for the rest of my (un)natural life, then after Christmas I might be able to do a plumbing course or something – anything – and start fixing the place. Pray it does not snow. And that I can find someone who wants to rent my Gran's house.

15th November.

It turns out 'impulse bought a house' means 'nothing happening soon' as the seller's solicitor is on holiday. The bank have created a few hundred extra forms just for me but despite clearly having the time to do this, they do not have anyone with the precise skills needed to help me struggle to fill even a single form in and I am not allowed to do it without someone staring at me, it turns out. It's all going to take everyone weeks, so the odds are I will still be here when the wiring is being done, and the boiler replaced and whatnot. Could I be looking forward to it any less?

16th November.

You think it can't get any worse and then you get a long letter, heavy on the guilt, in which your mother conveys her intention of spending Christmas with you and sends a list of all the things she does and does not want to eat over the festive period. I have sent her the advert I had for my ruin. Christmas will be spent here, in a tent, suggest you bring your own as mine is small. Christmas dinner will be baked beans served on a bed of overdone toast. If you want to add to that, it needs to be cooked already, edible raw, or something you can feasibly cook on a camping stove. This will go well, I can tell already.

17th November.

Letter from Isobel saying mummy has told her that I'm going to be hosting Christmas and should she buy some tree decorations as she imagines it is hard to get any fashionable ones out in the sticks. I have responded.

20th November.

I am officially the most horrible and unreasonable child in the history of ever. It's really no surprise that I've let the house fall down around me! And if I think she will solve my problems by bringing me food, I've got another think coming. Her life is very stressful just now and she foolishly thought she could count on me for much needed respite, but of course she should have known better. I always let her down. Obviously it took her a lot more words to make these points, but my mother does not believe in brevity. In fact she's always been at her most generous when telling me what she thinks.

22nd **November.**

Isobel has sent me a card. It says "Poor you, are you not even going to have a tree, then? Shame. Norway spruce are 'in' this year. I was in OK magazine at the weekend. I've enclosed a copy of the cutting as I thought it might cheer you up." You can't really see it's her. Mostly the image is of the one hit wonder who had passed out in her cleavage. Apparently he threw up on three different women that evening. Ah, what it is to move in glamorous circles. That moment when you realise that if you'd been mummy's darling favourite, it could have been you with a minor celebrity losing the plot in your arms. You too could have got a significant percentage of your tits in front of thousands of readers. But not your name. I find myself feeling really grateful for having been the irrelevant one, because however odd my life is, those are not my tits.

23rd **November.**

Twenty days since I last saw Evan. Twenty. I didn't mean for it to go on that long. Everything else went mad. What must he think? That I'm avoiding him – which I guess is true because I have been. That he scared me off? Did Evan scare me off? Haven't decided. Nervous about going back, certainly. Would feel awkward. What to say? How could it not be weird? And he knows where I live, he could have come down here any time and knocked on the door. Although he could have done that when I was out. I've never seen him off his own property. No car. No bike, even. I sound like a bunny boiler. It's just he's the only thing in my life that isn't 1) a ruined house 2) close family. I can't help but notice things about his life. I've never been good at making friends. Never really got the knack. He's one of the few people I've ever met who is weirder than me. An appealing quality in a person.

24th November.

Got my arse into gear and found a bottle of wine (mysterious that I had somehow bought and not emptied it). Peace offering/ talisman /weapon. I went to Wychelm. There he was. Easy. We just stood there in the open doorway, me in the rain unable to think of a single thing to say. He didn't say anything either. On it went. This long, tense, wet, what the fuck am I doing here silence. Eventually I managed to thrust the wine bottle at him and run away.

"Don't make me drink it all by myself," he shouted after me. "I'll get maudlin and lecherous which is a terrible combination."

I don't know where he gets his chat-up lines. "Maudlin and lecherous? Why didn't you say so before? What's not to like?" I was some way from the door by this point, shouting at him.

"You'll be safe if you drink at least half of the bottle."

I always fall for things like this. I don't know why. Totally impervious to style, class and wealth, invariably lured in by silliness.

So I stayed and I drank a lot of wine and talked a lot but I don't remember what was said. Mostly it was me talking so I guess my train wreck family featured a lot. I don't think he said much about himself. I meant to ask. Blame the wine. Blame the being easily led.

I did not end up in bed with him. Given my track record around half-hearted drunken sex with people I barely know, this seems like an important achievement. I woke up lying against him on the sofa, fully clothed. He smells like outside, earth and apples, woodsmoke. He breathes slower than I do. Two breaths for every one of mine is normal. Evan is not normal.

When he woke up I pointed out that he had not taken advantage of me.

"Tell me you're disappointed."

I said I was more relieved, which was tactless, but his being offended was definitely a pretence. He didn't sound hurt. Then he said, "Not my style. When you're burning for it, when you want me so badly you can't think about anything else, then."

He seemed very sure. That tone of voice. Remembering gives me goose bumps. "When?"

"When," he repeated. "But not any time soon, I don't think."

What to make of that? Don't know. Slept on his sofa the rest of the night. On my own. Mixed feelings. Wanting to be wanted, certainly. Not so hooked on him that the word 'burning' seems pertinent. And yet.

I guess I'm just not dealing with the consequences of not having made bad sex choices.

26th November.

Electricians next week. Paperwork moving. Seller's solicitor now back and in touch. Bank willing to let me see the forms it wants me to fill in. My solicitor has fallen down the stairs and broken a leg and might not make it back to the office before the start of the seasonal holidays, which I anticipate are long in the world of solicitors. It is now clear to me why these people charge so much for what they do. It is because they only work five hours a month. Gits. It's just a pile of bricks in the shape of a kitchen. Really, how hard can it be? People move house all the time, you'd think the process wouldn't be such a mystery to all of the professionals involved. Dear Gods!

29th November.

Can't bear being inside with the workmen. Went out and walked the perimeter of Evan's valley, for old time's sake. Now covered in mud – both me and the valley. Everything grey, damp and gloomy. Don't think it gets any sun at all at this time of the year. I'm finding the cold and the grey tough. Not like city winters at all. I'm used to 'alone in the crowd' lonely. Alone and alone turns out to be harder. Too much time with my own thoughts. Nothing to keep what's in my head in perspective. How would I know if I'd gone totally mad? How did my grandmother bear it, out here on her own for all those years? Can't imagine my father here as a child, or as a young man Can't really imagine my father at all right now.

30th November.

Asked Evan is if could use his garden to walk up the valley amongst the trees. He asked what I was looking for and I admitted to not really knowing. "Then the odds are you won't find it, but feel free."

I asked if that was the secret of the valley, that you have to know, or be clear about what you want from it. He said, "No, more a life thing. Hard to find what you don't know to be looking out for."

"Fair enough," says I. "So what is the secret of the valley?"

"If I told you then it wouldn't be secret, would it? I like it better when we talk about my moist cleft."

From there it was all bad puns and innuendo. Which felt oddly safe and familiar. I walked with him up to the edge of the trees. There's a small stream – no wonder with all the rain. We just stood about looking at things and I left not much the wiser. He's got a damp cleft and he doesn't like people entering it. And put that way, it seems totally fair enough.

1st December.

The good thing about living in a nameless cleft in a house full of plaster dust and workmen is that there is no Christmas. It cannot reach me here. The radio signal is patchy and not a single seasonal song gets through. There isn't a fairy light in sight, either. No forced jollity. It seems my neighbours are bah-humbugging people, or Satanists, or somewhere else and I love them for it. Perhaps I can hide here and pretend it's not happening.

3rd December.

Had a nightmare that my mother had turned up at the house. In the dream it was Christmas morning and she'd got Isobel with her, only Isobel was still a small child and screamed about everything if she didn't get her own way. We couldn't get across the living room to the rather tired looking Christmas tree (where did that come from?) because of all the slippery holly leaves on the floor. Living room strangely on a slope, and I was sliding down it helplessly while Isobel screamed about how she had to have all the best presents, and my mother recited the lists of things she would eat (including a horse) and would not eat (anything that came off a gingerbread house).

4th December.

Dear gods it's cold. Would it be wrong of me to try and seduce Evan on the off-chance his place is warmer? I bet he's warm, at any rate. I also bet he sleeps naked. Cannot imagine him in pyjamas. Have slept with people for worse reasons and it is very cold. I do sort of fancy him, which is odd. Don't normally find the male body inherently sexy. Suitable for my depraved purposes, yes. Sexy, not so much. It bothers me that I find him attractive, as though I am letting the side down.

6th December.

Visited my new ruin as I need to start planning this properly. Nervous, excited, hopeful. Trying to picture it fixed and work out what it ought to be like when it's done. If I get this right, there's more than money involved. It's a home. Someone could grow up in it, or grow old in it. Someone else's life will be shaped by what I make. I want it to be a good place. I'm starting to see how to make it work. I have a feeling that under all the awful fifties decorating, there's a much nicer house trying to get out. I've never really thought about houses having opinions about themselves before. May have been on my own for too long. May be more mad than I'd previously thought.

10th December.

Waved goodbye to the last of Gran's furniture today, so, indoor camping from here. I don't think she'd mind. What's gone was all simple, functional stuff – nothing of any great worth, nothing I had any reason to feel sentimental about either. Better to let the place unfurnished, I gather. Wiring all done, all evidence of previous wiring madness hidden forever. Mess mostly cleared. More cleaning yet to do. Paper to hang. Photographer coming from letting agent. It's all happening and it seems like I'm making it happen and I find that odd. I did not think I would be the sort of person to make anything much happen. Spent this afternoon in the garden, cutting back brambles and nettles. The smell of rotting fruit and leaves may be one of my favourite things ever. I like the feel of things in my hands, too. Tools, twigs, even brambles. Nothing ever felt this real before. I'm not who I was in London. I'm someone else here. Someone with dirty fingernails who hasn't bought a comfort hat in ages. Just the one woolly hat to keep my hair out of my face when I'm working! Was I this person all along but did not know, or has being here changed me?

15th December.

My mother arrived in an enormous car. Three suitcases and "I'll stay until the New Year," as greeting. Not seen that coming. How could I not have any furniture? How ridiculous. She disapproves of the colours I have chosen, the wallpaper patterns are dated and obvious. She hates the varnished floorboards, the kitchen is far too shabby and the garden is a mess. No one will want to buy this place from me. It's always educational getting to see my shortcomings through her eyes. I wish I could work up the enthusiasm to be cross about it, but there's no point arguing with her. She always knows best. I have heard a lot about what I ought to be doing in order to sell – the walls must be magnolia, that's what they say on all the television programs, apparently. I've not said anything about renting it out. Small victories. I had to give her the airbed, though. I have said very clearly that I am not buying furniture for her benefit and I don't want her to stay. She's capable of staying anyway purely out of spite. Best not to let her think I care too much either way. She can't stay until January that's for sure. I will kill her and bury her in the garden, god help me.

16th December.

I should get planning permission to double the size of this place because it's far too pokey for anyone to live in. I should knock it down and rebuild with something modern and chic. I must have a garage built, at least. Other cottages round here have garages. The kitchen is far too small and does not have any inbuilt gadgets. For the first time since I found out about the will, I think I understand why Gran left her house to me. I don't want to do all the things my mother thinks are vital. It would be wrong for the house, totally wrong for this land and this valley. Hard to believe that we're related at all, we're just so alien to each other, mother and I. She's still here. I've fed her beans on toast two meals running and she's still here. Why? What does she want? What is she trying to prove? There's more going on here than just spite, I think.

18th December.

I have a lodger lined up for January. The estate agent says they had barely put the photo in the window when someone came in and said it was exactly what they were looking for. Some kind of sabbatical, retreat type thing for six months. Perfect! My mother is furious and tells me I cannot rent the place out, but when challenged can offer no reason for saying this. She just doesn't like it. Or she doesn't like me doing things I haven't run past her for approval. I asked her outright why she was still there, sleeping on my airbed. I've had no proper decent sleep since she arrived, I feel like shit and I no longer feel like humouring her. After forty minutes (I timed her) of shouting accusations at me regarding what a useless, ungrateful and unhelpful sort of daughter I have always been, she admitted that she has fallen out with her most recent boyfriend and as a consequence has nowhere to live. Told her she can't stay here. There follows a twenty minute improvisation on the theme of I should be able to look after her for a few weeks in her time of need after she spent all those years lavishing all that time, care, attention and money on me. I told her to try that line on Isobel, because it wasn't going to work on me. My mother is still in my house. What if she won't go? Can she ruin everything? Will I have to get a court order to get her out like you have to do with squatters? How long does that take?

19ᵗʰ December.

She took her enormous car, and came back having bought a bed and some 'nice curtains' and a rug and cushions and has ordered a sofa. I can pay her back, she says. I totally lost it. I ended up screaming "You can't live here," at her, over and over again. I've signed a contract, I've rented the place out. I don't want this. "I'm only trying to help," she says, but she's not in the least bit interested in helping and she knows it. She just wants to push buttons. She wants to stay and will say anything that she thinks will get me to cave in. At least I've now got my airbed back, but I'm afraid to go to sleep. Afraid of what else she will do if I take my eyes off her for a moment. How do I make her leave without resorting to violence?

20ᵗʰ December.

Isobel has joined us for Christmas, because that was the plan, wasn't it? Just for a week or so. I said 'no' at the threshold and she literally pushed her way past me and into the house. I explained about the lodger, the almost no furniture. "Well, that's not very reasonable of you, is it?" she said. Cue me shouting repeatedly "I did not invite you to come here, go away," and suchlike for a long, long time. Even "fuck off out of my house," failed to get through.

"She's just being temperamental," my mother told Isobel. "The little tantrum will pass. Make yourself at home, Isobel. I hope you brought some Christmas decorations, this place really needs cheering up."

I walked out, which was risky. Stomped around in the dark for ages before my head cleared and I hauled a plan together. Went to Evan. Borrowed a can of paraffin and demanded that he kiss me.

"Didn't see that coming," he said.

"For courage," says I. "For not being crushed to death by my immediate family."

"That'll be with tongues then," he said.

What followed was too brief, sweet and dirty and basically me using him to get some sense of myself back. I think he knew and I don't think he minded in the least.

Took the paraffin, came back to the ancestral house. Said to immediate family "This is a can of paraffin and I'm going to take it back outside in a bit. You've got half an hour to get all your shit together and leave, or I am going to burn this place down with you in it. Is that perfectly clear?"

They went. Not before telling me that I'm sick and need medical assistance, probably need sectioning, but they went. What did I ever do to deserve this? Ongoing fear that it somehow me causing this. That I'm as useless as they say I am. Bad daughter for not giving this house to my mother in her moment of need. Bad daughter for not wanting them here for a festival that I hate and don't want to celebrate. I just want to be left alone. Is that so unreasonable? It's not like they're actually desperate – not if the cars they are both driving are anything to go by. At least the bed left with them. I feel cleaner now. I really am going to move out of here in the next few days, give all but one set of the keys over and start again. I liked being here, but I don't feel quiet and safe anymore. I feel violated. They know where I'm going, I just hope the pair of them will leave me alone.

Third Act: Twenty Eight

I invited the delectable Harri to check out a house with me. A nice daytrip, I thought. Maybe if I got lucky, a B&B somewhere. At the very least, time with Harri. Hours of it. Glorious!

Ruined farm, no access road. Empty for ages while the various people who'd inherited it failed to come up with anything, and then empty for longer because there's not actually much you can farm round here, and it's too small for a more industrial farming style, and too remote for a holiday home. Dirt cheap if I can pay for it up front, because they are absolutely desperate to sell it. The people I deal with are almost always desperate to sell. I buy the things no one in their right mind would want. I like that. So, it seemed like a good setup. Add in Harri, whose outrageous stories are always such a joy and it had the makings of a perfect day. Worth it for the stories if for nothing else. I've never encountered, much less courted anyone like Harri before and I have had no idea how to go about it, and that by itself has been impossible to resist, I've found.

Harry, Houri, Harriet, Harri... all these distinct and different people inside one skin and any time we meet up I don't know who he she they are going to be. No adequate pronouns exist. Irresistible. Fascinating and enigmatic, sexy beyond words with skin like summer twilight and dark brown eyes that hint at seduction and I must not fetishise the exotic because that's shitty but oh dear gods there has never been anyone this exotic in the world before. Sometimes when Harri looks at me it is as though they are seeing right into every pervy little dream I've ever entertained. Including my dreams of them. Harri looks into me and smiles the kind of smile to melt the underwear off a puritan. I am exposed, I think. Exposed and accepted, but it has not led to anything apart from the day trip.

I drive, and Harri tells me about a great uncle who was lost in a complicated ballooning accident in a mountain range I've never heard of. He came back twelve years later, unable or unwilling to ever speak a word of what had happened, but covered from the soles of his feet to the top of his head in tiny, beautiful tattoos. In his will, he left his skin to someone so they had to have him flayed before they could bury him. I hope the recipient was expecting the bequest. Imagine getting a totally tattoo covered entire human skin turn up unexpectedly in a parcel! It would be the most perfect act of revenge though.

So we parked up in what I am pretty sure was the right place and headed off down the unsurfaced farm track in search of the remains of the farmhouse. Harri calls me 'Katherine The Great' which I like so much that I've not yet admitted that my usual 'Kathy' is short for something else.

What other asides should I include now? I'm procrastinating. The sky was a most picture-perfect postcard shade of blue. The hedgerows were radiant and fragrant with flowers. The track – a soft yellow and stony was easy enough to walk along. Everything sounded of birdsong and smelled of plants. It's hard to come at this directly. I want to circle around what happened and creep up on it so that it does not get away from me. I want to pin it down even though I know what happens to butterflies pinned on collector's boards. They all go grey in the end. A butterfly that does not move is only part of what it means to be a butterfly. I do not want these memories to get dry, dusty, the wrong sort of mothy.

It was the childhood memory of a perfect summer's day, with buttercups bright and everything hopeful. There never were any real days like that, I am sure. Memory plays tricks on us all the time. We talked about how unnaturally perfect a day it seemed to be. Grasshoppers chirping, fox cubs glimpsed playing in a nearby field, more red and foxy than any other foxes I have ever seen. Uberfox. Ultimate fox. Perfect foxhood.

I'd only ever been in urban spaces with Harri before this trip. It turns out that there are even more Harris to find when you take them outside amongst wilder spaces. Harri who is part Aragorn from Tolkien and partly one of his elves, and a bit Druid priestess and a bit Merlin and more than a dash of Jain extremism thrown in for good measure. I've heard stories about monks who gently sweep the path before them to avoid killing anything, but I've never seen anyone do something like that before.

We stopped for every worm, snail, caterpillar – anything that had got itself into the wrong spot. We have to carry several caterpillars until Harri found the right plant for them. At the time I didn't even register what slow progress we must be making. It didn't matter. I forgot about the house we were going to look at. I just kept asking daft questions. "How do you know this stuff?" "How did you even see that?"

"What on earth is it, anyway?" "Are you David Attenborough in a really clever disguise?"

I can't remember the last time I felt this ignorant, and it didn't even bother me. Rare to be around someone who doesn't make a big deal out of what they know. I wish I could say that I felt like a child again, but my childhood was mostly about getting to feel stupid a lot, and this was different.

We stopped to untangle a sapling that had been bent over and trapped by a fallen branch. We stopped to move several stones that had fallen out of a wall and onto an ant's nest. We rescued a butterfly from a small puddle and Harri carried it on one hand until the brightly coloured wings dried out and it flew away. We took a detour across a field to where a deer had got itself tangled up in some old fence wire. I watched the frightened creature settle and grow still as Harri gently eased the wire away to set it free. Then it took off like a bullet and vanished in seconds.

A scream came from the far side of the meadow. Proper chilling stuff. I said something inane about it being our next rescue mission.

Harri said no.

"Why not?"

"Sounds like a rabbit. I guess a stoat got it."

"That's horrible. Poor bunny."

Harri shrugged. "Tough on the rabbit, fantastic news for the stoat. It's all about how you look at it, which is why I don't meddle."

"So the Saint Francis of Assisi routine is ok because?" Not my best line, but Harri laughed with good humour all the same.

"I like the Saint Francis thing. But look at it this way. The rocks don't need to be in the ants' nest. The puddle doesn't need the butterfly."

"Yoda of Assisi."

"There is nothing wrong with my grammar!"

And so we went back to the track and the almost forgotten quest for the farmhouse.

Harri said "Don't you know any fairy stories?"

I asked what that had to do with rescuing ants.

"If we run into a beautiful princess and the king will only let us marry her if we can separate a pound of poppy seeds from a pound of sesame seeds, we're going to need all the ant friends we can get."

"We're both marrying this princess, are we?"

"It's not obligatory, but I'm generally pro sharing."

"And you use ants for this sort of problem a lot, do you?"

"Not as often as you'd think, but I like to keep my ant karma high, just in case."

There followed a tale about a distant cousin who had ended up feeding their horse to a flock of ravens.

"Doesn't the horse get any say in this?" I asked.

"You'd think they should," said Harri, "But what really troubles me is the flock – you don't get flocks of ravens, just small family groups, so it must have been rooks or jackdaws lying about their classification to seem more important. Or something else entirely was going on there, but it certainly doesn't add up. Mind you, that cousin of mine is none too bright. His homing pigeons never came back, and that's not a euphemism."

Harri paused and treated me to one of those smiles that causes me to melt on the inside and risks me dripping puddles all over the ground. "Now you're a different sort of fairy story. Everything you touch turns to gold."

True enough. I've been preposterously lucky. "Some kind of capitalist fairy blew sparkle dust up my arse," I suggested.

"That could explain everything."

It could. I know how to say the right things about projections and market trends when talking to the lenders, but it's never been about the maths. Just gut feelings. Do I like a place? Is the land going to be unhappy if I build on it or change things? Does the land like me? Things you just don't mention to normal people. Things I could imagine explaining to Harri over a bottle of wine, though.

There was a wood fired bread oven standing by the side of the road. No sign of anyone, just us and the overgrown track, the bread oven and a singeing loaf of bread. Obviously we had to stop and rescue the load before it burned.

"Harri, does this sort of thing happen to you a lot?" I asked.

"What sort of thing?"

"Abandoned bread ovens in the middle of nowhere?"

Harri shrugged. "Well, not this specifically, obviously."

"But it doesn't seem weird to you?"

"No."

A worried look from Harri had me feeling that I'd just asked a really bad question. I didn't know how to put things right.

We turned a corner in the track and finally – voila – one missing farmhouse. Except this one had washing on the line and smoke coming from the chimney.

We'd been looking for a ruin. I got the map out and it started to rain. Heavy drops of water out of the clear sky, turning the garden into a rainbow sheen of colours. Harri ran off to rescue the laundry and I put the map away and stared at the uncanny colours.

A woman came out of the farmhouse, all smiles and thanks for Harri, who had taken the laundry into the porch. "That was you who took the bread from my oven and set my poor deer free, wasn't it?" she said. Well yes, it was, but how did she know? It had been a weird sort of day, but we turned a corner at this point, I think. At the time it didn't seem such a big deal.

The old woman spoke only to Harri. "So I will tell you that if you jump into my well, you will find what you've been looking for."

Harri looked at me, long, and hard, for what felt like a very long time. I just stood there like a lemon. The whole thing was so loopy that I didn't take it seriously.

"Would you jump into a well with me?" Harri asked, deadpan.

I said something stupid about liking them, but not enough to break my ankles in the middle of nowhere.

"Even if there was going to be magic and adventure on the other side?" Harri asked.

"There's going to be water, and pain," I said. "You're taking the piss, right?"

Before I could think or act or ask or anything useful, Harri thanked the woman and headed to the well. It was a proper fairytale well with a little wall and a little roof. Harri sat on the wall and looked back at me. "You're sure you won't come?"

"You're mad. No, I'll stay put to haul you out afterwards or call an ambulance or whatever. Have you got heat stroke or something?" I was starting to panic, but not enough to do anything useful.

Harri looked disappointed. They turned away from me, gazed into the well, and then simply dropped down. I waited for the splash, or the cry of pain on impact, or a shout. Something. Anything. The silence was oppressive. I walked over to the well but it felt like walking through treacle, everything in slow motion and impossible. Inside the well there were bricks, with moss growing in the gaps. There was water a little way down, I couldn't see the bottom. I shouted, and waited, and shouted some more. I kept trying to think of something to do that would help, but I couldn't come up with anything. I was afraid Harri had died, knocked unconscious and drowned but there was no way of getting down there aside from jumping and me diving in too was hardly going to help.

The minutes mounted up, and Harri did not emerge or call out or float to the surface. I'd been holding my breath, and when my lungs were bursting, I knew that was it, that Harri couldn't possibly have survived the fall. I think I was in shock. Couldn't move. Couldn't cry.

The woman from the farmhouse came over to me. "Throw yourself in too, if you like, for what good it will do you. Quick enough to help yourself, but not so much use to anyone else, are you? You get what you deserve round here."

I wanted to say "that's not fair," and I wanted to ask what had happened to Harri and hear anything that wasn't terminal. I also wanted to curse the bitch for getting us into this whole mess, but at the same time I wanted her to help me get Harri out of the well so I could hardly mouth off at her. So I stayed as I was, still and silent.

"You get what you're looking for," the woman said, and she walked away from me.

I stood there for I don't know how long. I stood there until the light faded and what was next to me was just the ruined shell of an old house with the door all rotted and vines growing out of the roof. The building I was looking for in the first place.

What had happened? I didn't know how to think about it, how to make sense of anything. I stood there and stood there and the farmhouse stayed a ruin and Harri stayed missing and nothing made sense to me. It left me hollow on the inside and unable to trust the ground to stay put beneath my feet.

And then what?

Time, and car journeys. Blurs of misery, guilt and confusion. Knowing I should call someone, tell someone. But who to call? And what to say? If Harri had a family I had no idea where they were. If Harri had a surname or an address – well, I didn't know those either. Were there friends closer than me? Lovers? I don't know. It shocks me how much I don't know. Call the police and describe the event? I imagined trying to explain, and could not see how to do it. I'd be certified. Blamed. I've written it all down and as I sit here I can imagine the police coming calling, and taking my journals as evidence. The police do not come. Nothing has happened as a result of Harri disappearing. No one I know asks me about Harri. It's like they never were.

Now that I look back, there are so many gaps in this that it frightens me. Was I not paying attention? When did we first meet? Where? I can't pinpoint anything. Harri was around, on the edges of my modest social life, an irresistible smile. I remember thinking when we started talking that it was as though we'd always been talking and here was someone who got me in a way most people don't. Someone who had already seen inside of me and liked what they found. When? Last year? Before my birthday? Or further back? Why wasn't I paying more attention?

Harri did everything so easily around people it seemed like they knew everyone. Or was it just that casual charm in action, and everyone playing along? We all know Harri. We all want to know Harri and so we nod and smile and say yes, of course, Harri is a friend of mine, in the hopes that saying so makes it true. And for a while, it was true. But they slip away as easily, leaving nothing but my confusion in their wake. A dream of a person, forgotten now by everyone but me. No one asks after Harri. No one wonders why we haven't seen Harri in a while. I have this irrational feeling that they were only here for me, and that's why I can remember but no one else does. As though Harri never really existed for anyone else. As if I imagined it all. I read my own words describing what happened and it seems like total madness. But it is what I remember.

I have bought the farmhouse – well, the buying is in progress at any rate. I had to do it. A feeling of obligation and also of need, and there is no one I have to justify myself to. I need to know what happened, and where Harri went, and as I'm not willing to throw myself into the well, all I can do is stay near the well and wait. Of course, I've been away a while, things could have changed without me. I just have to hope this is a meaningful course of action.

I had the obligatory structural survey done. The verdict was – knock it down and start again. Unsafe and beyond rescue. I've brought a caravan over. I can pretend to be working on the building and thus live on the land. No one will check, not out here. It looks like a ruin. I can't square what's here now with what was here on the day Harri disappeared. I sit on the rim of the well and look at the still, dark water going who knows how far down? I think about jumping. I've though about it every day I've been here. I think if I jumped I would break bones, and either drown straight off or lie at the bottom of the well until cold or hunger did for me. Like an Aztec human sacrifice in a cenote, only with no gods lined up to be appeased by the proceedings. I would disappear in my own way, but without magic.

If I was sure I could follow Harri, would I jump then? A jump that depends on certainty is not an act of faith. I think that matters.

Twilight. I don't know what time it was. Sat on the caravan step, watching the shadows grow and the bats come out. Little, furtive explorative flappings. I've got to know their habits rather well. Airborne night mice.

There was no drama in the air. Nothing happened to announce the change. One moment a ruin, the next a fully functional, inhabited farmhouse. Smoke in the chimney, washing on the line. Chickens scratching around the door and a smell of fresh bread. I sat there for a long time, wondering what, if anything, to do.

"Still here?" asked the old woman. I hadn't even seen her approach me, she just turned up. "Still waiting, are you?"

I asked her if she knew what had happened to Harri.

"Your friend who jumped in the well?"

"Yes."

"No idea."

That may of course have been true.

"You are not welcome here, you do not belong. Go away." She turned her back on me after saying this, and stalked back into the house, and as she passed through the front door, the house reverted into its previous, dilapidated state.

I knew before she said – I don't sleep well here. I know I'm not welcome, but I will stay and wait, and figure this out.

For the last couple of days, I have been pretending to be Harri. I've wandered about fixing walls, and looking for things to rescue. So far there have been no bread ovens, no piles of poppy and sesame seeds that need separating out. There are some jackdaws who seem moderately interested in me. I've put food out for them. They seem more friendly than anything else around here. It's a start. I will not be beaten by this place. I am good at land, usually. My entire business and life is based on how good I am at working with the land. I will learn how this place works. I will stay and I will figure out what to do.

I dreamed that a worm had made its home in a fold in the skin of my left leg. It kept growing, and I could see it but I couldn't feel it. I could even see it moving about, but there were no sensations, like it wasn't my leg at all. I felt like I ought to be able to feel something. I wanted to wash it out, but had no clean water. When I woke up, it felt as though the worm really was in my leg, but now I can't see it. Washing does not help. The only time I talk to ordinary, normal people is when I go shopping. The people I thought were friends have not got in touch, and I've not phoned any of them. Writing is a different kind of silence, but there's some comfort in it. If I can wrap words around life then I still have some sort of grip on things. I am not entirely lost.

I saw the bread oven today. There was no bread in it, and the whole thing was totally cold. I know it wasn't in that spot yesterday, and it has gone now. It looked to me like a laughing open mouth. A person can read too much into these things, I know. I've borrowed every fairytale book the library has. Harri liked these stories, talked about them, told me off for not knowing about them. Maybe they have a value, or a relevance that I'm not aware of. So far I have learned about how a sausage can marry a mouse, and how a little tailor can win against giants. I learn about Mother Holle and her bread oven and laundry and what she does to young women. Is this Mother Holle's house superimposing itself over the farmhouse? Why would it show up here? I learn that good manners are important and that direct questions seldom get any good results. I learn that you can make a pact with the devil and not lose your soul if you happen to be clever enough or get the right help. I do not earn where Harri is, but I learn what happens to lazy, good for nothing second sisters who jump into wells. I do not think it would ever have been a good idea for me to jump in there.

Once upon a time, there were two sisters. The first sister had long, golden locks that gleamed like the sun. She was graceful and beautiful and good at a great many things and so she was much loved and greatly praised. The second sister however was dark haired and awkward and people called her funny looking and it was generally understood that no one could love her and that no one would marry her. The golden sister would do golden things. Pearls would fall from her lips. Gold would be showered upon her. Princes would seek her hand and offer to kill things, and each other, for her sake. Golden all the way.

The second sister failed at everything she tried for many years. Shit came out of her mouth and shit was showered upon her and instead of princes, she got her bum pinched by strangers who considered it to be a good joke.

But then the mysterious and witchy granny died in strange circumstances and left her wolf-haunted cottage to the second sister. Perhaps granny herself had been a wolf all along. It explains her living arrangements. Woodland grandmothers in sugar frosted houses, waiting for children to eat. Woodland grandmothers in chicken legged cottages with skulls around the door instead of roses. Grandmother love is full of tests and challenges. Perhaps it is rightly for the second sisters, for the dark ones and not the golden children.

Granny's house in the woods, where you must go when they leave you to starve. Eat or be eaten. Kill or be killed.

They see the golden daughter come back from her adventures covered in what looks like gold, and they never ask if something pissed on her. They see the dark daughter come back covered in shit, and they take it as a measure of her worth. They do not ask what she had to do, or why. I think I understand a few things now about myself that I had never seen clearly before.

Patience pays off. I take the bread from the oven before it burns, and I eat all of it. Smells like perfection, tastes like nothing. Pretend bread, fairy tale bread. Bait for the trap. The good and golden sister will keep the bread safe and return it to its rightful owner. I eat it. Every last crumb. I am not the golden daughter come to do as I am told. I am the other kind. I come on my own terms and I want Harri safe, and I will fight you for this land, and for my lost friend, and I will win.

The crow says "Hey, lady, I could eat a horse." I said it was cat food, so some of it probably had been horse, once. "Jeez babe, it's a metaphor, you people are always so literal."

I've had some kind of summer flu. Don't really know what day it is. I've been falling in and out of sleep a lot. I could turn the radio on and find out when I am, but I haven't done so yet. There's something about feeling I'm outside of time that I like. Probably I am still a bit feverish and mad. All magic depends on fungi, on the networks they create in the soil. This is what really makes all the important connections between all things and if you can talk to the fungi, and hear the fungi, then basically you can do anything.

Already this idea seems less convincing to me than it did when I first woke up.

One day I will be a proper grownup and will no longer have to eat baked beans out of a tin, with a spoon. Or is that as unrealistic as talking to the fungi?

I've started talking to everything, not just the crows. Trees. Fungi in the soil. The sky. The well. Even the house. Only the crows are talking back at the moment, and mostly what they have to say is about food, or shiny things, or what the wind is doing. Either crows are easier to understand than other things, or I miss all the subtext. I guess trees are going to be going at a much slower pace. I need to learn how to listen slowly to them, and how to listen faster for insects and whatnot. Everything moves in its own timeframe.

I just asked the well 'what are you?' but I realise that assumes it is one thing and not a collection of lots of things (bricks, moss, water, stone, drop, space etc). Is a well one thing, or many things? What am I? Blood, bones, teeth, hair, skin, but that's not an answer. I need to understand the well. Perhaps these are things it can't tell me because I'm asking the wrong questions. Does this, of itself mean I am making progress in understanding the well?

A garden is a human imposition on a bit of land. I do not have to turn this jungle back into a garden. It is not my job to pick fruit and take in otherworldly laundry. This is the job of the good sister who is good because she belongs to the domestic sphere and doesn't get ideas. She tidies things up. I am the second sister. I am the lazy and self-serving one, but so is the sunbathing fox on the flagstones. So are the frogs loitering about in the pond. Nothing here works for the sake of it and nothing here longs for useful employment. I do not see how any of this insight is going to help Harri, but what if Harri does not need to be helped?

The ants have plenty enough to do staying alive. What kind of sick bastard mixes up two different kinds of seeds to see if you've got any ant friends who have the time and energy to sort it out for you? The fairytales are all about forms of virtue I find I don't much like. Why waste ant friends on pointless seed sorting? Why assume they are supposed to show such massive gratitude for some rather small human gesture? I would get my ant army to take the farmhouse apart, in their own time and I'd pay them in jam. As I don't have an ant army, I'll have to do it myself. Mother Domestic Virtues can get stuffed.

I've been working flat out these last three days, moving everything that was loose and easily moved. A pile for floorboards and wainscoting, a pile for debris, another for bricks. I could do with scaffolding, kit, extra hands, tools, experience. Stupid to be doing this, but satisfying all the same. It's an old house, old enough to have been made with very little technology, but with far more manpower, I assume. Anything can be unmade.

Today, being the fourth day, the unmaker rests – or at least goes shopping and books into a B&B overnight so as to have a bath and a check in with consensus reality. I am clean as I write this, which is a noteworthy occasion, and the rest of reality behaving exactly as expected and has other people cooking food in it. And the uncreator looked upon the cooking and saw that it was good.

Bricks neatly stacked in one pile, wood in another. Debris pile is a mess, but the farmhouse has been reduced to its component parts. Ant army? Magical fungi? Elves who climbed out of the well during the night but who must disappear before the first cock crows? They have yet to invoice me, so I don't know who is responsible. This probably ought to worry me. I'm not sure why it doesn't.

Shadows lengthen. I watch the ghost of a farmhouse slide in and out of focus, as a faint voice reaches me. "You bitch. You evil, sneaky, vicious little bitch."

I have won this round, at least.

"Obviously we would like a horse."

"A whole one."

"Dead – otherwise the running around is something of a bother."

"Not too freshly dead, either, for the texture."

"And the flavour, come to that."

"You can't over-weather a horse, I always say."

"You can, because if you leave it too long the bugs get all the good bits and just leave you with bones."

Such is my life. I have a selection of rooks, crows and jackdaws now, and what they really want, is a horse.

"We'll do wonderful things for you, after the horse."

But they won't say exactly what sort of things, and I suspect them of lying. If I had a dead horse going spare, that would be one thing, but I'm not killing a horse for them.

I had to hire a guy with a landrover and a trailer to get the rubble out. "Bloody waste, if you ask me," he said. I hadn't asked him. "Bits of this place were a thousand years old and more." I would have saved it if I could. I don't think he believed me when I said so. "Not your history though, is it, love? Not your ancestors, not your land. You English. You think you can own it all." I've heard it before, and it's not just a race issue. Older people in villages resent change. I've saved a fair few buildings along the way, but it doesn't count for much. It's not just the bricks. A house is made of stories, too. Without them, a house is just a shell. What I have now is all stories and no house – perhaps there's an answer in that.

The new farmhouse is tiny and mostly made of wood, and stands on the site of the old hearth. I've used bits and pieces from the original building to make this, and it follows my understanding of how the original, this-world farmhouse must have looked. Not the ruin I bought, but the oldest part of the house based on what's in my copy of the deeds. It's been in the same family for hundreds of years, passed down. Never once sold until I bought it. But there's nothing to tell me how, or why or when Mother Holle rolled in.

It took a few days of waiting before she showed up at the new house. Tiny laundry dangling from a hair's thickness of washing line. Chickens no bigger than woodlice carry on unperturbed. Smoke in the chimney. Out of the door she came. "It's the wrong size," she said, looking up at me, clearly irate. The size difference did not seem to unnerve her, only to annoy.

I picked the house up. A hunch, nothing more. She screamed at me to put it back down at once. I'm not sure how she comes and goes but it has more to do with the ground than with the house itself. This magic does not quite accommodate me holding the house off the ground, in my hands.

I asked her every question I could think of about who she is where she came from, the well, and Harri. She was evasive and said a lot of things that made little sense to me. However, I expect there's some truth in there somewhere so I'm going to try and record it accurately so that I don't forget.

Her house is not the farmhouse, except that sometimes it is. They are totally different and occasionally the same. The well is also like this, sometimes it will just be a well with a frog or two at the bottom – princely or otherwise. Sometimes the well is something else. A person who understands these things can travel "with the ebb and flow." She said "ebb and flow" more than once in different contexts. As though there's a natural underlying pattern to how places connect and disconnect. At least I think that's what we're talking about.

There are big tides that take a long time and little ebbs and flows that are more like days. The house and the well do not have the same tides. Other places may be like this, too.

So my instinct not to jump in the well may have been good. It may have been a regular well for me simply because the timing was wrong. Perhaps one day this will change. I'll worry about what to do if I notice this has happened – not sure how I am to tell.

I now think I may have got a bit carried away with the whole bad sister thing. It may not be that simple.

It may be less about good girls getting to pass through and bad ones getting shit dropped on them, and more about the tides. The critical question may not be about my virtue, but whether I can learn to feel what the tides are doing. How long do I need to stay here in order to figure out whether I can do this?

The last thing she said to me was really odd. It was about Harri. "You're asking all the wrong questions. You have to ask what Harri is, not where they are."

She waited until my hands were shaking to say that. I was a second away from having to put the house back down on the ground and did not have chance to ask any further questions. If I understand things correctly then she will be back because she has no control over it. So long as there is some sort of building here, the tide will bring her in and out just as it's done for who knows how long.

I'm finding all this tidal stuff hard to get to grips with, but for now am going to treat it as true and see what happens. For it to make sense, there has to be some kind of parallel worlds system going on. Well, semi-parallel. Sometimes parallel. Moving in and out of relationship with each other. That's a brain-hurting sort of idea.

There's one thing that really bothers me, and it's how she said 'Harri'. Not to sound like Harry or Harriet, but with more of an 'O' to it. Like she'd swapped the vowels over so it came out more like Hiray. Only with more 'o'. It's not an accent thing entirely. What is Hiray? Perhaps this is the question.

There's a Welsh word – Hiraeth – it means a specifically Welsh kind of homesickness. I do not think Harri was Welsh. They did not sound Welsh, or even mention it. I don't know anything about Harri's family or where they came from. I'm not sure hiraeth is it, but it's all I've come up with so far. It wasn't Hooray, either, although it sounded a bit like that. It's the only clue I have right now, and I see no way to go anywhere with it.

I ask the well about tides and timings, and what it is when it isn't being a well. It was a one-sided conversation. Then there was a voice from the bottom, a little voice, and it said "If you drop something precious in here then I can bring it back for you, and when I do, I too will be changed into something you want."

"Are you Harri?" I asked the voice, even though it sounds nothing like them.

"I am a Harri. I could be your Harri." As it was speaking I could feel that it and the well were not the same. Something dropped now would have more interesting consequences. I did not throw myself in, but dropped a penny and made a wish to better understand what's happening here.

"Do you want this shiny thing back?" the voice asked.

I declined.

Woke up in the middle of the night, in pain. Reason: Pea under mattress. Not like the marrowfat peas I've been eating out of tins. About the size of my fist, which is far, far too big for a pea. But otherwise, there's no question as to what it is. Under my mattress, for fuck's sake! It wasn't there when I went to bed, I could hardly have failed to notice it. The caravan door is not locked, but who would creep in here at night to stuff a giant pea underneath me? I am not a heavy sleeper, either.

By the time I'd made my first coffee, the pea had sprouted where I'd sat it on the draining board. I have taken it outside, in self defence. A pea plant of that scale is not a pea for interior deployment.

I think we all know what sort of pea this is. I know, and so do you, dear imaginary friends and witnesses to my raging insanity. I could kill it now, before it grows up in search of giant cloud kingdoms. Peas are, when you get down to it, pulses. There's not much to choose between a giant peastalk and a giant beanstalk.

Lunchtime. Its taller than the caravan now, and has two leaves.

"Someone trade you that?" the crows ask.

"Thought magic beans were right out of fashion."

"Bloody hipster retro magic if you ask me."

"Did you really fall for the bean scam?"

I told them it just turned up, and they made what for crows is the equivalent of tutting noises. This particular sound foxed me for ages – I thought they were choking, but I get it now.

"Can't be good news, that sort of bean,"

"Things like that don't just turn up, something turns them up."

"They could have turned themselves up."

"I resent attributing agency to peas, be they magical or otherwise."

"Magical pea plants are people too!"

"I can't stand a fluffy corvid."

They bicker a lot. Any excuse. I have to listen because they are at present the best source of information I have, and I need to keep track in case there turns out to be something important in their chatter. I've never been good at people. Hanging out with crows is in some ways easier, but still mostly confusing.

Tomorrow, when I wake up, there will be a pea stalk that reaches into the clouds, I just know it. I will have to decide what I am going to do.

Of course what I didn't think about at the time is that a pea plant is not a one way system. Things may go down as well as up your pea and if giant peas had smallprint, that detail would be tucked in some obscure paragraph on the nineteenth page of the terms and conditions. People choosing to live in the shadow of giant peas do so at their own risk. The pea provider takes no responsibility for where your pea goes or the ways in which it might act as a bridge. Anyone climbing the pea does so at their own risk and pea climbing insurance policies are not available at this time. Pea climbing may also invalidate other insurance policies. Always check with your provider. A giant pea showing up in your bed may or may not be considered an act of god.

I slept through the events of the night, and really whatever came down the beanstalk cannot have been small and should not have been quiet. That it, or they, did not stand on my caravan seems to be nothing short of a miracle. The whole area looks like something you'd expect in footage from the aftermath of a natural disaster. The enormous pea stalk is just fine, though. The caravan and my miniature farmhouse for Mother Holle survived unscathed. For as far as I have dared to check, the ground looks like it's been shelled. Trees are splinters, wall and fences are heaps and broken lines.

I climbed into a couple of the 'shell holes' trying to make sense of the carnage. From the inside, looking at the contours I had to wonder if they were footprints. Other people might not have felt any obligation to wonder anything of the sort.

"Giant beanstalk, stands to reason you've got a giant infestation, sweetheart."

I asked the crows if the mess looked like footprints from above. I sort of wish I hadn't.

"Five of them at least. Trolls, if you ask me. Too broad proportional to the width for your regular giant feet."

"Nah, it's Elder Gods, I tell you. Just count the toes for yourself."

I followed the tracks. I think it was just one set, at least once it got away from my caravan. Maybe there had been others. Maybe some of them climbed back up. The trail was not hard to follow – a zigzag of mayhem through the fields. Frightened cows trying to hide. Other cows that had clearly been chewed on as snacks. No signs of any irate farmers – or had they been eaten too? No sign of the military. Where are the helicopters and swat teams when you need them? How can no one else have noticed this happening?

I've had the radio on for local news. Nothing. Conspiracy? Cover up? Further proof of my own insanity? "Who benefits, when there's a beanstalk?" I ask the crows. "If the beanstalk is a scam, like you said, who gets the payoff?"

"Not us."

"Definitely not us."

"Someone else."

"Wait until the giant is distracted and go in for the gold."

"The second mouse gets the cheese. And we get the first mouse."

I mentioned all the cow remains in the next valley and they claimed innocence. Should I have trusted them so much?

Climbing beanstalks, or pea stalks, or I rather imagine, any other monstrously overgrown garden vegetable, is not as easy as advertised. A person does not, I would like it to be known, simply get up in the morning, observe the enormous and recently grown legume and then just climb it. Ropes, crampons, ice axes – things of that ilk are required. The stalk of a giant pea is fundamentally slippery in nature, rather too vertical and not possessed of sufficient footholds. You could be forgiven for thinking that they were not designed with human climbing in mind at all. Even if I had any of the gear, I lack the skills to safely use it.

The other development I wasn't expecting, are the suitably gigantic pea flowers. Will there be massive bees along to pollinate them? And when the peas are ripe – well, I know what over-ripe pea pods do is explode. I do not know quite what direction all this is moving in. At current rate, exploding peas and new giant pea stalks are not many days away. Still no one else seems to have noticed any of this.

I think there were bees in the night. I think I was awake, and not dreaming. Oddly what I remember most today is not the sound of them, but the smell. I can't even say what it was like. It wasn't like anything else. I do not want there to be giant bees in the giant peas.

I did not dream them. I know because the pea pods are now forming so evidently something came to pollinate them. I stood outside for a while and watched them get larger and fatter. I've since packed a bag and run away. I'm in a B&B some miles from the caravan, trying to pass myself off as normal, and watching the news. The pea pods will split soon, there will be a pea bombardment from on high – I don't know how far they could go. Then there will be a forest of giant peas around the caravan reaching to who knows where and making a bridge for who knows what.

Was it always like that at the farmhouse? Did they cope, through the generations who lived on that land, with trolls, beans, and half eaten cows? It's not as if they can tell anyone now. These are the sorts of details estate agents always leave out.

I walked up a hill behind the town to a popular beauty spot. Lots of cars and picnics. I could see where the farm is because there's now a forest of giant beanstalks over there, as anticipated. All of them reach into the clouds. Hundreds of them. I could see things with wings flapping between the plants. Not bees, that's about all I can say.

I accosted a man and asked him what he thought of the view.

"Lovely day for it," he said. "Marvellous colours. Makes me wish I could paint."

I asked him what he thought about the beanstalks and whether there's a lot of that sort of thing round here. More desperation on my part than anything else.

"Stare too long into the void, and the void may stare back at you," he said.

"That's not a void, that's a forest of giant peas!"

"The same rules can be assumed to apply," he said. He seemed entirely cheerful about it. "If I don't bother them, I'm sure they won't bother me."

I asked him whether he worried about giants. He looked me up and down and said, "You're not from around here, are you?" It was pretty obvious that he didn't want to talk to me after that.

What if the tidal thing is true? What if the tide went out and took me with it and washed me up somewhere else when I wasn't paying attention? How would I be able to tell if that had happened? What if Harri jumped into the well that day not to leave, but to stay? What if I am the one who left? A bit of human flotsam on the uncanny tide. That moment when you look around at the munchkins and consider that you might not be in Kansas anymore. I think I exist. My money exists here at any rate. Or someone's money does and I am able to access it. Is this some sort of parallel world, is there another me here? Dear Gods, this is worse than giants trampling about in the night. This is my whole reality. I'm not sure what I believe right now.

I do exist here. There is a me who is not me. I am a socialite icon and the paparazzi follow me round. Photos of me turn up in glossy magazines, and I have seen them, and it is deeply disconcerting. My sister is a very popular journalist – emphasis on the pop, not the journalism. I am a multi-millionaire property developer and trend setter. I have just set the media on fire by suggesting that shabby tweed can be sexy and that the naked male chin is a bit unsettling and should not be encouraged. I am spending my money, and sooner or later I suspect that I will notice this and will probably assume some kind of identity theft has been perpetrated and get the police involved. That's going to take some explaining.

I have loaded my car (this car, a car...) with non-perishable supplies I can see no option but to go back to the caravan and hope that whatever deposited me here will eventually take me somewhere else. Maybe even back where I came from. It's logical to think that tides go in and out. None of this is logical. I have a magazine full of my face as evidence. Not to prove anything to anyone else, just to try and prove this to me. The existence of another me makes me feel very nervous indeed. Even the 'me' word starts to feel untrustworthy.

I go back to the bean forest. It smells like the memory of wholefood shops from a distant phase of my childhood. I am trying to remember when on earth I could have gone into a wholefood shop. Sacks of dried beans and mystery flours. Is some other me somehow seeping in? I'm sure my mother never went in for all of that.

The crows say, "You're a bit fucked, aren't you, doll?"

And I say, "Yes, yes I am."

"What you need, is a wizard."

"A proper wizard, mind, none of your pointy hat, silly title, no demonology skills worth mentioning kind of wizard."

"Not one of the unlucky ones, either."

"Terrible things, unlucky wizards, and a bugger to get rid of as well. Worse than mites."

I ventured a question: "Why would a wizard help me right now?"

"See, they know about stuff."

"And things."

"Very clever, wizards."

I suppose I could go forth in search of a wizard. Perhaps in these parts it would just be a case of checking the classified ads or the posters at the library. Perhaps if a person waits until the wind is blowing the right ways and shouts 'I need a wizard' they can hear you and turn up. I'm having trouble knowing what to take seriously today. I could just stay here and wait for the next pea fall, which by the looks of things may be more like a landslide, and if I survive that, who knows what will come down from the next crop of peas?

Or I find a wizard. A person I have no means of identifying and no means of recompensing, who may not exist in the first place, and whose willingness to help me remains unknown. What do I want? I'd say I want to go home, except home has always been a hypothetical idea for me. I'd settle for somewhere to belong, somewhere that feels passably safe.

My conclusion is that I do not need to find a wizard. I need to become a wizard. This is a far more ludicrous line of thought than anything the crows have suggested, but I find it strangely appealing. Still, finding a wizard could make becoming a wizard a good deal easier.

I asked the crows if any of them knew of any actual wizards.

"There's that one up on the mountain who turned herself into a tree. Not so talkative these days, mind."

"Do you remember the one with the dog?"

"Didn't he die of exposure?"

"I think we ate him, once he'd softened up."

"Hopeless lot, unlucky wizards."

"There is Merryweather."

"I thought Merryweather was dead?"

"Only ever a story, that one, or so I heard."

I have a name. It is a place to start.

I went back to the library that loaned my all the fairy tale books – same one, thankfully. Awkwardness avoided. I started poking about, and once you get past the first room, there's another room full of dusty books you only imagine should be in libraries but don't normally see a few shelves down from The Very Hungry Caterpillar. Hard to make sense of the filing though. Odd what's made it through, and what hasn't. Lots of Maurice Sendak. No Enid Blyton. I feel reassured by this. Books about wizards that may or may not be works of fiction. Books about wars I've never heard of. Places I've never heard of. It's all rather distracting. There are Merryweather references all over the place. There's something of the Robin Hood vibe about Merryweather, something that rings true but isn't proven. Merryweather strides the worlds, setting wrongs to right. Incredibly powerful, but a decent person with it. Merryweather has castles, and boats, a flying carpet, and a bookshop in Gloucester. Which seems pretty weird to me. Oddly close to home. But, assuming this Gloucester is somewhere akin to where I left my previous one, I could be on to something.

Bookends, it turns out, is an entirely empty building with boarded up windows and not any kind of wizard-occupied bookshop at all. From the name I infer that it was a bookshop once. On seeing it, I realised that I had of course seen it before, and it was entirely boarded up then, too. This Gloucester is more familiar than not with its mix of once decent but now largely messed up historical architecture surrounded by people who have the tuned out qualities of glue sniffers.

What caught my eye though was a chap sat outside Bookends and paying the building serious attention, as though if he didn't keep watching someone might pocket it and run off. He was wearing the kind of bright green that does not ask to be ignored. It took me a while to work out what, aside from the extraordinary shade, seemed odd about him. It was the droopy ears. Big, fluffy things like you'd expect to find on a lop-eared rabbit. I only realised when he cocked one up to listen to something. I walked over and asked if he knew where I could find Merryweather.

"Alas, if only. One can but wait and hope. Wait and hope."

"Have you been here long?" I asked.

"Three years, two months, seventeen days and forty five minutes," he said. "He could be back any time now."

"The place looks pretty empty," says I.

"Yes, but when Merryweather returns, the entire bookshop will return as well. This is the way of it, I believe."

"Tidal, then?"

His already large eyes went very big at these words. "You know?"

"I'm not from here. The tide washed me in. I thought perhaps Merryweather could help me."

The rabbit man clasped my hands in his and made a lot of excited, but otherwise incomprehensible noises for several minutes, culminating in "I do believe the tide has finally turned!"

I thought tides changed all the time and said as much.

"Oh, little ebbs and flows, certainly, but the big one is slow, and marvellous and I shall live to see the world go mad." He seemed oddly cheerful about the process.

I sat with him until it got dark – really dark – no streetlights in this part of town. Apparently the rabbit guy had just been sitting in this same spot for three years, two months, seventeen days and some hours without moving at all, which raises some serious questions about his biology. I suggested we break into the building – I was bored.

"What if there's nothing in there?" he said.

"Then we leave again?"

"No, I mean really nothing, as to say, the absence of everything."

"Is that likely?" I asked.

"It seems logical to expect as much."

Why? He thought it was self evident. I find that a cold bum is a great motivator at times. This is the wisdom statement I mean to leave to posterity. When I could bear the cold, hard pavement no more, I headed in. There's a side alley – part of the tourist trail where I come from, because if you can get down there and bend yourself awkwardly, you can sort of make out the facade of a really old house, which used to face something other than the bricks next door. There was no alley here, but there was a really rotten looking fence, so I took my chances and gave it a kick. It wobbled and on the third go a plank gave way and one of its friends relented a bit. I made my entry hole and squeezed through.

On the other side of the fence I found a neatly laid-out garden with little box hedges and giant topiary in shapes too peculiar to adequately describe. A mediaeval bestiary gone mad. Forget the snakes head on a leopard's body routine. More things you've never seen before with the head of another thing you've never seen before that's clearly way out of proportion leading to the sense that here are two troubling things that should never have been put together in the first place. At least, I hope they were made up.

From this side, the house looked nothing at all like the bookshop facing out onto the street. Also, there were lights in the windows where no light should have been. I went back into the street and checked – there was no light in the bookshop. Given where the windows were, this did not add up at all. I told the rabbit guy that he might want to take a look.

"I have sworn to sit here until Merryweather returns."

So I left him to it.

The front door to the house opened before I even managed to knock on it. Although there seemed to be no one doing the opening. I followed the light into a room full of people. People-ish may be a more accurate term. Odd even by the standards of my Gloucester, although less prone to using 'fuck' as a form of audio punctuation. They all turned to look at me, and they all started asking questions, and it went something like this...

"Are you Merryweather?"

"We've been waiting to see you for ages."

"I was told to ask..."

"I hope you don't mind, but..."

"... with an oversized turnip and a puddle."

"...started it..."

And so on and so forth, making less and less sense for a long time before they stopped being so excited that there was no point my even trying to speak.

"I'm not Merryweather. I'm Kathleen Sylvia West. I'm looking for Merryweather too."

"West is a good omen. They always come from out of the west, don't they?"

"Are you sure you aren't Merryweather?"

I said I was quite sure, but this didn't seem to persuade them.

"Really? You see one of the things we've been wondering, as we've waited, is if one of us might have been Merryweather all along and just not known it."

"How could you possibly not know something like that?" I asked. "Merryweather is a legend. You couldn't be a legend and not know, surely?"

"Well, how do you know who you are? How can you be sure that anything you think you remember is really true? Why wouldn't you be Merryweather?"

They invited me to stay with them, but I didn't take them up on it. I had a feeling that it was a sort of a trap, that it was a place of not doing anything and it would be all too easy to end up like my friend with the rabbit ears, just sitting there. Or worse, talking myself out of what shreds of identity I've hung on to. How do you know that what you remember of who you are is real? For fuck's sake, if you can't trust your own memory, what is there? Reality seems increasingly fragile and I want to take care of it, and keep what little of it I have left.

I slept in the car. I feel like a large, hairy animal killed itself on my face during the night, and my back is clearly full of angry rocks. I have eaten cold baked beans with a spoon. It troubles me to realise that these beans may be the only familiar things left in my life.

So there's the house and there is the bookshop, and there is no wizard. Clearly the house does not occupy the same reality as the bookshop. One or the other is really somewhere else, they just overlap weirdly. I want to get inside, but I'm not sure which one to go for. I want to understand. Not be chucked around randomly by forces I don't even see coming. I want to do this deliberately. I can only take what I can carry and there is no knowing if I'm off for an hour, a year, or the rest of my life. It feels like the right thing to do, and that's all I have to go on.

Right. I have packed. I have eaten all the perishable things not packed. I have moved the car to what looks like an empty lot. I am going out – I may be some time. I feel like I should put a date in here to mark the occasion, but I don't know what the date is. If you find this journal, you're going to have to guess how long I've been gone, from the state of the car and its contents. In fairness I must point out to you that at the point of my departure, the car already looks like it's been abandoned for about a month.

If the evidence suggests to you that I'm not long gone, I hope you'll be kind enough to leave my stuff alone. If I've clearly been gone for ages, do as you see fit because that probably means I'm not coming back. In case of my absence, there is no one you can contact. I come from another world, I have no legal existence here and if there is anyone who would mourn my passing (which I doubt) you have no way of getting a message to them anyway.

I am going into Bookends, looking for Merryweather. If you are reading this, then I have very likely failed in my quest.

That's a suitably pessimistic and melodramatic point from which to start out on an adventure, isn't it? I shall miss you most of all, diary. If I am still sane, it is in no small part thanks to you. Please don't blame yourself if it turns out I was quite mad all along.

Chapter four, such as it is: Thirty-Five

My mother was thirty-five when I was born. An old mother for her generation. I'd never really thought about having or not having children until now. Today, I am thirty-five. And mostly I haven't had children. Happy birthday to me. Sat in a car I had no reason to think I'd ever see again, writing this in a musty old book, wondering what to say about life, and who I am saying it to. Hello future me, this is how things are right now.

The truth changes all the time. Usually in small ways. What I think is true now may not seem true tomorrow. I have walked between worlds. I will write down all the things that seem to be true at the moment. I will write them on the off-chance a future me finds this helpful.

The worlds are many, but I still think they are finite. They are not parallel worlds, although the ones closest to each other are most alike. We may find versions of ourselves, and versions of things we know, or we may not. The tide is coming in, and everything is changing.

The tide is slow, and does not follow easily observed patterns, but this is what I've got so far. When two places are brought together by the tide, a number of things can happen. The places may embrace each other, creating a larger, composite reality. The places may collide, creating an explosion or a combustion. Earthquakes are often manifestations of this. At the smaller scale, objects and people who collide can just go up in flames. Repeat incidents of spontaneous combustions – human and otherwise – indicate tidal action. When places or things are very different from each other, they tend to embrace. The more alike things are, the higher the risk of mutual destruction.

This is where the whole issue of wizards enters the equation. In finding that which is almost but not quite yourself, in facing the moment of possible annihilation, there is great power. The weaker self may smoulder and collapse, and if the stronger self can capitalise on this unravelling, they can absorb the life, the being, the power of the weaker one. Of course both may explode, or implode, mistakes can be made, death may not be instant. I have heard a great many stories now, no two quite the same.

When you take another version of yourself inside you, their stories, their lives and knowledge become part of who you are. A bit like the ghosts of our former selves, carried in memory, only more uneasy even than these. People we might have been, nearly were, who will always resent what's been stolen from them. This is no doubt why the vast majority of wizards seem to be such bitter, unhappy creatures.

The person who can become all of their possible selves from all possible worlds, will achieve a status of unthinkable power. The knowledge of all the worlds is theirs. A person who can become some of their selves, becomes a wizard, and grows in power. It is the body knowledge of multiple worlds that does it, I think. A wizard does not control the tides, but they can navigate them like a skilled sailor. To continue the metaphor, where a sailor crosses great distances, sails into the wind at will, harvests fish and caries treasures and cargo, so the wizard may do many things that others who cannot navigate the tides, cannot do.

There is a point of beginning for a wizard, some means to find another version of self. I don't know much about how this has happened for others, but evidently it must start somewhere, and likely more by chance than design the first time. There are ways of moving between worlds, and as the tide comes in, opportunities for collision increase.

To become a wizard is a terrible thing. The person who chooses the path risks collisions and annihilation at every turn. The one who would be a wizard seeks themselves out, overcomes themself, becomes themself, destroys, embraces, consumes. Remembers more lives than they have lived. Fights with themselves to hold on to one sane, coherent identity from the array of shattered voices inside their own head. Power and self-loathing go hand in hand.

I am thirty-five years of age. This I know as a fact. I was lucky in that the first few mes I found were small, lost, cowardly things. I possessed and crushed them, absorbed their lives while discarding the wispy personas that went with them. They were detestable. It may be easier to kill yourself in pursuit of wizardry if you also hate yourself. There are few wizards in the worlds – most explode along the way. What few there are, generally turn out to be evil. Obsessed with power, they are willing to keep on killing themselves in order to get more of it.

How did I know what to do, the first time? Facing a mirror image of myself, feeling my skin prickle and burn, seeing the smoke billowing from her pores... what did I do, and how did I do it? The only analogy

I can think of is sex. There is life before sex, and life after it, and before you have no way of knowing or really imagining. Somehow, in all your ignorance you make the transition anyway because there is a knowledge in your body that takes over from your mind. Do we all have it in us to eat our other selves? Or is this a body knowledge that only turns up in some? I don't know.

My grandmother exploded, on the inside. It took her a while to die. From what I know now, more than one of my grandmothers died that way, and all at about the same time. I do not think this is a coincidence. It may have been an accident of course. Did they set out to converge, or was it just an effect of the tide? I have one memory of a grandmother who lived. If I can work out which one of me pertains to her, in which world, then perhaps I have a grandmother who is also a wizard. It would be good to have someone to talk to.

Grandmother's house. We all go back there in the end. Fact.

Merryweather may or may not be true. The stories span worlds. The legend of the one truly good wizard get everywhere – perhaps only because people want to believe it could happen. I've found a fair few of those legends now, and read them. They're funny things. The Merryweather stories are not, for the greater part, anything to do with Merryweather at all. I know nothing about the life, history, personality etc of Merryweather, only that they are a good wizard. Just a background character who rocks up in other people's stories at critical moments to help, offer advice and generally be useful and benevolent. The real hero is always someone else. The main action is always somewhere Merryweather is not.

I've been to places I just don't have the language to describe. Places that feel, smell, taste other than anything my life had prepared me for. How do I talk about the texture of the wind, or the energy of the soil? I have consumed myself in more than a dozen permutations. I have seen a great deal too much of who I could have been, and I have become them, too, even as I loathed them. I have travelled beyond time and reason. I have also stood at threshold places where I could hear the sound of the shifting tides, flowing, washing, pushing, changing everything. I can step between worlds at will now, although mostly I have no idea where I'm going. In all of this, so many things have lost their meaning for me. I am an array of ghosts captured in a single meat sack. I am becoming a wizard. I think that with time, and enough power I will be able to feel like a coherent person again.

I am not jaded about the wonders of the worlds, although I realise it might sound that way, to imaginary future me. I do not know why finding Merryweather has seemed so important, when I have looked for so long and found so little. The drive is still in me. I do know why finding a surviving grandmother matters to me. I have to work out which one she was, before the tide washes her away or she hits another grandmother and blows up. First, I have to collect the me I left here, before I knew what I was doing.

Dear Gods, this 'me' was offensive. Too close for comfort as well. A developer, like I set out to be, only successful and ruthless. Making money out of money. Would I have been her if I'd carried on? Turning quiet valleys into executive developments for other assholes burdened with too much success. It makes me sick.

I found me in an exclusive watering hole on the edge of a second homes village full of gigantic cars and pale children. Actual servants. The hunting is all about proximity and I can feel the pull of another me from miles away, now I've had some practice. A buzzing of the skin that becomes more of a burning feeling the closer I get. A vicious ache in my bones. It is essential to stay calm and focused when this kicks off in earnest, and to approach the prey slowly. There's a knack to not exploding. I got lucky the first time, but these days I am a lot more in control.

I know how to hold my edges securely when it feels like everything I am is trying to fall apart. Breathe steadily. Refuse to yield. It has to be a slow approach when going in for the kill, so as to absorb the shocks proximity creates. The more they look like me, the tougher it is going to be. Similarity creates combustion and makes survival considerably harder. This one looked exactly like me, only smug. I watched her face for a while as I moved in. Annoyed resentment. I stepped closer. Offended.

Step.

Angry.

Step.

Afraid.

Step.

Really afraid and in pain.

Step.

No sense of recognition at all. I put a hand on her bare, tanned shoulder and watched the smoke rise around my fingers and the flames dance over her skin. I felt my own body yearn towards the same destruction, but I held, I refused to succumb. I felt her essence, her sordid, money-grabbing little life poured into me and I crushed it into useful crumbs with very little effort.

Most of the mes are so weak. They are narrow, and self-absorbed. It is easy to hate us.

There were friends with this one. Darkly attired women with the airbrushed aesthetic of the wealthy. One of them screamed. No one tried to stop me. They just stared at me as I walked away from the smouldering place their companion had occupied. Just a drift of smoke and a nasty, dark smear on the posh cushions. I expect they can afford the years of counselling this is going to require.

I'd meant to rest here for a while before going back over previous kills to find the grandmother who did not explode. I need time to draw breath. But, there is another me here. I can feel it. I assume this means another wanderer between worlds. Possibly a me who means to master the tides. It does not bode well. Are they strong enough to take me? How much more dangerous must it be to try and take someone who has already eaten other lives? If we're well matched, does that make explosion inevitable? I've not heard of anything like this before, it could be a first.

I've been on the move all day. I can feel the other me getting closer, and then further away, but definitely trying to head in my direction. Sensing me as I sense them, no doubt. Hunting me, for sure. I'm lucky that I have a car here, they clearly do too from the speed they can move at. Or they have way more magic at their command than I do. I can't drive forever. Too tired already, not safe, having to take a break. Afraid to stand and fight this tired. Can't concentrate enough to do anything. Do not dare go to sleep, either. Have to find an overlap point and slip away. Can't orientate. Can't feel where the tide pulls. Does this other me not get tired at all? What the hell am I up against here?

There are places that are like tidal pools, or like causeways that vanish at high tides. Paths you can't use when the tide is in. They come and go, in their own cycles and often connected to the same geographical area. These cycles can take minutes, or year. One of the things a magician does is find these points and times of overlap to use them. But to become a magician you have to first pass between the worlds by accident and absorb one of your other selves. Which raises some questions about how a person gets started. I wonder sometimes if the tide has its own mind and intentions. If so, the tide itself is God. Would a God of the Tides respond to prayers of petition? Perhaps so. Right now I find that idea easy to believe because I have found a crossing point and slipped through, and I felt the path wash away behind me as a small tide came in. The deep ocean of reality has chosen to bless me, today, against all the odds. I have escaped, I have survived and I do not know why. It is a great relief to no longer feel hunted.

I find myself in an empty world in human terms. The only sounds are of the wind and the birds. I have walked all day and seen no roads, no planes, and no signs of human habitation or other even slightly human-ish activity. There are a great many birds, most of which are wholly unfamiliar. I wonder if there is a bird me? I've not felt anything, but I'm so tired that I'm not sure I would, especially not if it was subtle. Lots of silence, and the sighing of wind in the long grasses. Vast expanses of open sky. I'm not carrying much – the life saving tin of beans, the emergency chocolate. I have no idea how to live off the land. I found a stream and it tasted okay, which I hope is a good sign. Where are the fairy bread ovens when you need them?

If the tide has its own intentions and intelligence, why did it send me here? Come to that, why would it want me rampaging though its many worlds, killing myself at frequent intervals along the way? The whole point of magicians is being able to mess with the tides for personal gain. Why would the tides choose to go along with that? What's in it for them? Or are they setting us up in some way that is invisible to us so as to use us for the things they cannot do directly themselves? Things involving the use of feet and the availability of opposable thumbs, perhaps. There can be none of the obvious human motives at play here, for sure. What could a tide want? What other purpose could my actions serve? Could what's happening to me be controlled or directed by some force beyond me? Have I been deluding myself all along? Also, I am very hungry and too cold to risk sleeping and my fire is crap and I think there was a snake earlier. I can't feel anything out there and I don't know where to go next or what to do.

Mushrooms for breakfast! Wonderful, tasty happiness. It may also be why this place now has so many tiny, pretty fairy things in it and why the rocks are singing eighties soft rock classics. But, I feel much better regardless of what's caused it. Who knew otherworldly rocks were so into Bon Jovi?

Those fairy tales about standing stones going down to nearby streams for a drink? Disconcerting in practice.

Dear tides, is there perhaps a world I could go to where there's a lot of free food and some kind of naturally occurring duvet plants? Or a world where I can fly, or suddenly, magically know how to do lots of useful outdoorsy survival type things? I mention this because the tiny sour apples worked out worse than the mushrooms. I'm now really glad there's no one else here because no one can see all the undignified sudden crapping in the bushes that has featured today.

If I was truly a magician who could control the tides, I would be able to choose my destination, and go there by force of will alone. I would not be shuffled about randomly. If I was a magician, or a wizard or whatever we want to call it today, I would likely also have a better idea of where to go from here. A land flowing in coffee and baked beans would be nice.

Ok, not a land flowing in coffee and baked beans. Bad idea. Although I think 'ominous stewy sea' is a better description of what I've got. Still, something probably thinks this is all very funny, and the thing that thinks it is most assuredly not me. There is stuff in my pores that should not be there and I will smell of it forever.

I'm being followed again. I don't know if it's the same me as before, or a different one. It doesn't matter because I'm just too tired to keep running away. Nothing to fight with. Expecting to lose. Resigned to it, really. I suppose I've not had such a bad life. Lives, even. And maybe when I'm eaten, it won't seem like the end. Maybe I'll go on living inside the mind of the me who wins. I just hope it doesn't hurt too much. None of my victims have seemed to enjoy it.

I'm clearly not a narcissist because I have never enjoyed looking at my own face. I'm usually a bit of a disappointment to myself, even in mirrors. It is so much worse when the face is scaled up five times or so. The crookedness of my teeth looks worse than ever. The moles with hairs on them, on the underside of my chin where I normally manage not to look. The scars, pock marks, the spots. I never thought of myself as pretty, but on this scale, with every fault writ large, I'm pretty shocking.

And not dead. I've been noticing that about me all day. I did smoke at the extremities for a while. I'm sore, but not ash. Hold a safe proximity for long enough and it turns out that the options start to change.

This other me exists at a different pace. Words are scarce, but we have a truce of non-consumption and are swapping notes. Slowly. Giant me has something living in her toenails, and keeps picking giant snot jellyfish globules out of her nose. There have been mes I've felt considerably less kinship with. She's just said "For my people," and stopped again. There's a wasp's nest in her ear, I've just noticed. "Working with." Now we're looking at the sky. "The tectonic plate logic of interconnected and overlapping multipliants of reality."

Note to self. Do not make assumptions about other mes. We are full of surprises.

"It's about harmonious presence and attunement coupled with logical understanding."

Oh gee, why did I never think of this?

"Reading the fluctuations through study."

Um.

"To travel by will and..."

The suspense is now killing me.

"Survive both the convergences and the rifts of separation."

Places converging must be really messy. I can't begin to imagine what the pulling apart is like, but it could even be worse. I think this tide must be unpleasant, if it has any self awareness and intentions at all. Maybe this is why it likes me.

When giant me had done talking, she left, looking for other versions of us to try and persuade to take up a path on non-violence. I'm not sure what I think of this at the moment. Glad to be alive, above and beyond all else.

Mostly I travel with the intention of finding and destroying myself. I've not previously tried to be more specific about where I'm going, or to try and move about for other reasons. It makes me realise just how focused and obsessed I've been with the whole becoming a wizard thing, and maybe it is time to change tack. In me is the memory of a grandmother who did not explode. It's not a clear memory, we weren't close in that version of things either, and as she lived, I did not have the connection with her that came from inheriting the house. There's a thread of feeling, though. Ghost memories from a me who lived a small, sad life and never knew how to love or desire anyone else. That incarnation –a Katy – feared grandmother, and particularly feared her judgement and criticism. A steady refrain of "well, I wouldn't have done it like that," haunts those recollections.

My family are not nice people. It would have been too much to hope for a world alternative enough to throw up one of those warm hearted, flower growing, cake making, lavender scented and bountiful grandmothers. If there is any justice, the non-exploding grandmother will turn out to have skulls on her fence posts and a cottage wandering about on chicken legs. Of late I've been finding it helps to have wholly unrealistic expectations.

Now I'm finding out about her, I feel for this lost and eaten version of myself. I can taste the life I consumed, the flavour and sense of it is all there. Lives belong to the places that hold them and through that I can feel the nature of the place that once held this life. I understand everything. This is why we must destroy ourselves, to claim the body knowledge of the many worlds, and then feel our way between them. Otherwise, the only movement comes from chance or the whim of the tides. Is destruction the only way, or could there be other paths that allow deliberate crossings? What if there are reasons other than power, for being a magician? Perhaps I'm getting soft in my old age.

I never come in too close at the beginning. I think landing right next to myself could prove fatal. Plus you never know what you're walking into or who exactly you might be dealing with. This is not just about the issue of how colliding with yourself generally causes explosions and spontaneous human combustion. It's better to get a feel for my intended victim, and a sense of whether they are powerful enough to pose any threat.

So with this in mind I step across to be somewhere near the grandmother, but not too close so that I can take a proper measure before I expose myself to any risks. I take a basket, out of respect for the grandmother stories and because I'm a great believer in bribery. A selection of small bottles of spirits, a cake, a bottle of lavender perfume. A scarf. As soon as I cross the threshold, I know exactly where she is.

As introductions go this is going to be interesting. I've eaten her granddaughter. Will she be able to tell? Am I the wolf in this story? What big eyes you have, granddaughter. All the better to peer into the cracks in reality with, my dear. Time to walk. Through woods, obviously.

The place felt achingly familiar, but looked like nowhere I'd ever seen before. It took me a while to figure out what was going on. This of course is not the ancestral home of my reality, in its tiny, weird hamlet. This version offered me just the one house, stood at the neck of the valley and surrounded entirely by trees.

I knocked on the door, all psyched up for a familial encounter, and Evan opened it. My Evan. Not an otherworldly version of him, I swear, but absolutely the same person. He recognised me and asked why I was there. I explained that I was looking for my grandmother. He said he'd always thought I would figure it out eventually, but I don't know what he thought I'd figured. He told me the grandmother wasn't in, but was somewhere in the valley. Then he asked me in. He was shifty and odd, and an idea occurred to me.

"Evan, are you shagging my grandmother?"

He smiled, with what looked like no apparent shame but some mild discomfort, and said yes.

"Evan, were you shagging my other grandmother as well?" He didn't turn a hair at the question, although I was fighting down a blush.

"Well, only until she died, obviously."

The thing is, he hasn't changed at all. He looks exactly the way I remember him, smells how I remember him. I've changed though, because the degree to which I want him is now something I find disconcerting. It makes conversations difficult. It makes thinking difficult. I asked him how many generations of my family he'd managed to shag. He clearly had to think about this one.

"None of the men," he said, "So I've missed a couple of generations."

"And not me," I pointed out.

He grinned. "Yet."

That really annoys me. The inclination's there, granted, but the mental image of him humping my grandmother is a bit more than I can deal with.

"You aren't my granddaughter. I don't know who you are, but I'm not at all sure I want you in my house."

Memorable family reunion number one hundred and ninety six. Evan spoke up for me, and thanks to him, I got to stay for a while. I didn't feel any great rush of recognition, affection or belonging. It's perhaps as well.

"Wizardry runs in your family," Evan said. "You've all got some degree of knack for it, and most generations, somewhere, one of you goes around eating all the others, so the lines of heredity get a bit odd. It's happened enough times that you really are only one family in a way that's rather rare." He directed the next bit to the grandmother. "Your mother ate her great grandmother. She ate your granddaughter. That makes you..." he paused as though trying to find a good word for that kind of relationship. "It makes you family, doesn't it?"

"I never ate anybody," she said defensively. I think she was lying, or just prefers to think of it in different terms.

"I ate a lot of people," I said. Obviously it all went well from there.

"I know what you're up to, Evan, but kin by cannibalism or not, I won't share and I can't teach her."

Suit yourself," said Evan, as though it was really the old woman's loss that she wasn't going to do what he wanted. Then he suggested I just step across into the version of this house where I'd first found it. "Stay the night," he said. "You look like you need a rest."

When was anyone last kind to me?

I slept for four hours. Awake now in the middle of the night. My body feels more at peace for being back where it belongs. I hadn't realised that before, the tension that comes when I'm somewhere else, the relief of being here. I'm not sure where Evan is – perhaps that's as well. I'm feeling so much rage and frustration realising that I've spent years on this strange and lonely journey only to find out that he knew about everything all along, it was all here and he never said a bloody word to me. There's no fucking place like home, eh Dorothy? Except of course all the other places that are almost exactly like home.

Evan brought me breakfast in bed. This redeems him somewhat. We talked – mostly about the immediate things, the house, the valley, my grandmothers. Well, I talked and he evaded a lot, although it didn't seem like that at the time. I can't think of one useful new detail I've squeezed out of him.

Why is there only one of you? Did you eat yourself?

"There was only ever one of me."

Does that have anything to do with why the valley is so peculiar?

"Why do you think it's weird? Seems fine to me"

Why don't you get any older?

"Didn't seem worth the effort."

What are you?

"That's a very personal question if you don't mind."

What am I supposed to do now?

"Well, that's a much more interesting question, isn't it? What do you want to do?"

I don't know.

What's going on with you and my other grandmother and the teaching thing? What were you asking her to teach me?

"It's a moot point now, as she won't. Mostly selfish bastards, your family."

I know. I expect I'm much the same.

"You could choose otherwise."

And do what? Give me some options.

"We could go for a walk," he said.

"Where?"

"The valley of course."

Dear diary, I am going into the valley, with Evan. Don't wait up for me.

The trick to thinking about the valley is to consider it as something that is folded, both in space and time. There are many more paths that lead to it than can be seen from outside. It is easier to make sense of it now I've had some experience of moving myself about in complicated ways. Even so, I still find it a challenge. When I've been here before, all I've done is take the path of least resistance. Going the easy way puts you on a time path that spends many hours going nowhere. Resist that pull, and other paths become discernible, and there are other places within the valley to explore. There's beauty and wildness. Ancient trees abound, with vast, gnarled trunks, and an intense feeling of presence. Evan says there are all sorts of things living here but not to expect to see them. They are not sociable. He's different once he's out in the valley. More complicated. More real.

I asked him why he was shagging his way through my family, and he said that's not it at all. It's more the case that we've been shagging our way through him. Why are we doing that? He wishes he could ascribe it wholly to his innate sexiness, but the truth is that the valley is a place of power and he is the key to it. I'm surprised he told me that, but it's not like I'm going to screw him to get into this place. The only reason to bed Evan would be for the sheer pleasure of doing it.

I asked him what happened to all the other wizards in my family. They all exploded, eventually. Sooner or later they ran into another version of themselves who also wanted to be a magician. The more powerful people are, the bigger the risk. I guess power can also be a point of similarity, and the more power you have, the harder it can be to control, he says. I've not found that, but its early days yet. When I told him about the giant me, and how we didn't destroy each other, he seemed both surprised and hopeful. I think something really unusual happened there.

At one point, in one of the warmer times – or is it places? – we got naked to splash about in a vast, clear pool together. There was of course a waterfall somewhere nearby and the sound of it, along with birdsong, filled the air. It was a strangely not-sexual period of time. Very naked, and honest, but there was also something reverential about. I think that came from the atmosphere of the pool itself, the deep sense of peace in the place. Light on water creating its own magic. It felt like me stopping, stepping out of the rush of things for a while, and I don't do that very often.

The more I hear about what my family are, and what they do, the less I want to continue along this path I've been following. It's like the line of least resistance through the valley – it seems easy, but it goes nowhere. I think there must be other paths, less obvious ones with more potential. I don't want to just chase power until it kills me, and the novelty of trying to become a wizard has worn off.

My grandmother, the one who is most truly my own, warned me about not trying to control Evan.

It's funny, I remember the conversation with her clearly, but I can't remember when or where it happened. I didn't even see Evan until months after her death. I can't imagine being inclined to use him sexually in the hopes that would be a means to getting control of the valley. He who cannot be bothered to age, and who is so clearly a part of the land itself. And what is this land? Complicated, layered and folded, but not tidal, I think. This is the shore. This is the point the tide comes in and to, or from. Whatever he is, he and this place are profoundly connected.

I choose to do better. I choose not to use him or to seek for control of this place. I choose to find something other than the path of least resistance.

While we were sat naked together, I did my best to explain my intentions to him. I want him to know I'm not like all the others. He was cautious, but not cynical.

"You certainly could be different," he said. "I could be persuaded to believe in you. If you want it, you could be Merryweather, even."

"Isn't Merryweather already Merryweather?" I asked.

He asked me what I thought Merryweather was and I said there was clearly a myth and a collection of stories but maybe a real person, or even more than one person those myths were based on in the first place.

"Merryweather is stories, and I made them up." This was the most serious I have ever seen him. "I made Merryweather up. And I wrote most of the stories and seeded them across the worlds. It was just something to amuse myself with when it started, but it's gained its own momentum."

I hadn't seen that coming. He told me how much he wanted there to be something to believe in, some source of hope. I asked if this is because what mostly magicians do is essentially shit, and he said that was the short answer.

"And you think I could be Merryweather for you?"

"It's never seemed worth having this conversation with anyone else."

"What about the bookshop? There are people waiting for Merryweather, in a building Merryweather supposedly owns, doesn't that mean he's out there somewhere?"

"Bookends? I own it. You can have it if you want the job."

I'm going to need some time to think about all this. It's a bit unexpected, but I was looking for a different path.

Whatever Evan is, he is not a magician. There is no wizardry in what he does. I think he's a part of where the tides come in. There used, he said, to be more places like this. More points of stability and more people who existed to hold that calm and provide safe havens. There used to be gentler tides and a far easier shifting of possibilities as places drifted towards each other, or away again. What he talks about sounds like a richer, wilder kind of reality. More dangerous in some ways, but far more generous and interesting as well. As the tides have grown more violent, some places have become extinct, while others are changed by the energy of what's happening.

Power for the sake of power. I've been on that path a while now and I understand what it is and what it does. It was absolutely intoxicating at first. Like being drunk and reaching compulsively for the next shot glass and not thinking about the hangover the next day. But like any other addiction, every act of consumption is a little bit less rewarding than the previous time. My appreciation for the rush declines. Evan says there are other ways to take and that most wizards figure this out after a while. A magician, he tells me, can generally be measured by their capacity for destruction. The power to take creates the power to take even more. Until you bite off more reality than you can successfully chew and swallow, and then you explode.

I don't want to fall into someone else's story. Evan is charming, in an earthy, filthy kind of way, but I don't just want to step into this role he's created. It all sounds far too heroic, for a start. Too grandiose, too important. Not just save the world, save the complex, shifting mesh of many worlds. Undo the damage done to the tides themselves by people with far more power than I would dare to have. No pressure, then! How could I bear such a role? How could I even get up in the morning with that kind of burden on my shoulders?

I've also got a feeling that the person who sets off determined to save the worlds and put everything right, is going to turn out to be just as destructive as any other magician out there. It's an inhuman idea. I'd have to be some kind of raving ego-maniac to fancy my chances of pulling it off. I'm many things that I am not especially proud of, but not that. Even with all the mes I've eaten, I'm not an ego on legs. Saving the world is not on my agenda. I'm looking for some smaller and more realistic niche to occupy.

We talked for hours, and I cried a lot, which feels distinctly out of character. Apparently there were all sorts of things I'd not grieved, or dealt with and they all came pouring out in a mess of snot and blubbering. Better out than in, I suppose. Wet and non-fatal explosions may be the better way forward.

I'm starting to realise just how very invested Evan is in his vision of the restorative hero mage, and just how much he wants that to be me. In some ways it's touching, but, I'm not doing it. He's spent lifetimes on this. So, I won't shag him, I won't save him, I won't be the hero he's dreamed of. Where do we go from there? He's one of the few people who makes any kind of sense to me and with whom I feel kinship and empathy. I am set on being the most monumental let-down for him. There's nowhere to go with this.

I went to see my mother. Isn't that what's supposed to happen when your life is in transition and you need someone who can hear you out, and maybe give a shit? Time smoothes things over, knocks out the details, creates illusions. There are so many things I hadn't remembered – like the intensity of noise in London, the confusing nature of buses. The deep joy that is the specialist hat shop. The dirty, gritty feel of skin after a few hours on the streets.

How do you walk back into another person's life after nearly eight years of absence? Only when I reached the city did it occur to me that she could be dead, or moved. I might not be able to find her. How do I describe the feeling of dislocation that gave me? The ambiguity in my heart. I eventually remembered that last time I saw her she was between men and abodes. I no longer knew where she lived, so I thought I'd see if Isobel had stayed put.

Neither dead nor absent, the utter familiarity of my mother when I arrived at Isobel's home was almost overwhelming. Still in the same atmosphere and decor, only with Isobel in the mix. My sister is between jobs, resting. There was also a lodger called Geoff, about whom I know nothing. Isobel, a silent, uncanny ghost of herself now, with all the colour washed out of her. Managing to look undernourished and puffy all at once, her eyes have become pits in her face. No one could call her the pretty one now, and I feel remorselessly good about this.

Mother – dyed, painted, botoxed and surgically rearranged to be just the same as ever, only perpetually a bit surprised looking. Not a woman, but a museum piece, badly stuffed. Failed taxidermy in motion. The creature of my B movie nightmares. Between them they create an effect that I find wholly unpleasant.

There was no anger or curiosity expressed over my long absence, only sneering dismissal. She supposed I'd been too ashamed to show my face all this time. She knows perfectly well what I do, how sad my little life is, what a failure I've been. I decided not to tell her a thing. I do not need her approval or her goodwill. I'm not sure what I do need or even why I went, but it felt necessary. A check-in with the past. A point of reference.

Poor Isobel has been unlucky of late, I was told. Unlucky in love. Unlucky in not getting the roles she really deserved and having to make do with bit part work and being an extra just to pay the bills. Unlucky with her face, too which clearly wasn't helping her work prospects. She really should go under the knife, my mother thinks. It's her only hope now. I am glad not to be Isobel, and not to be living with those opinions.

I am glad I am not and never was the chosen one. My face is my own. In other worlds, there are other mothers, more and less kind. Other sisters, more and less useless. I have half memories of them. Not a single one of my mothers really knows who fathered her children. I'm not sure many of my fathers know, either. This father, I learned, is still very much alive, as self-absorbed as ever. His life revolves around his PR, his legacy his public profile. I've looked him up and the art is also much the same as ever – too clever and heartless, long on explanations short on inherent worth or beauty. You can see the magician in him.

Part of me wants to seek him out and ask about his mother, and his family history on that side. Does he know what's in his blood? Part of me knows what would happen if I tried and I don't want to get sucked back into his mind games. I'm more forgiving of my mother than of him – she's a fuckup, but its honest narcissism at heart. He's a whole other kind of creature. He's far too much like me, when you get down to it. All we can do is find subtle ways to fight each other for moments of power. I want it to be otherwise, but what, realistically, can he teach me that I'd find it in my interests to learn?

I'm pulling in the old threads of my life. Tying off loose ends. Thinking about the past and the future in terms of my life and the bigger picture. We are how we live. We are what we do. So, what am I doing? Where do I go from here?"

There is a well in the valley. I must have seen it before, but previously 'well' meant one of those cottage garden things, with a neat brick surround, a cute little roof and a bucket. Plus I had no idea that wells were significant. There's no wall around this one, no drop and no bucket. Instead, there's a pale, exposed sandy area and the water bubbles up through it. I thought technically that was a spring. Evan tells me there is no real difference, not where it matters.

I'm no expert on wells, just somewhat haunted by them. I've spent a while sitting with this one, trying to figure it out. Wells, tides, transition points, being a magician, the fluidity to move between places, seeping like the water does. It almost makes sense. Evan says I can stay as long as I want, sleep as much as I need to (which is to say, a lot). I know he's hoping if I stay he can work on me to persuade me to be Merryweather. He's fairly transparent. The tension has eased between us now that it's clear that I'm not going to use him – well, aside from staying here, but he offered so that's different. There is still attraction, but I can't look at him without seeing how he's been treated and I just don't want to add to that. Given my background, could he ever see me as anything other than a colonial invader?

Today I started planning what to take and this has made me realise that I mean to go. Not with ambitions to play out, but because there are things I need to learn. Whatever the knowledge costs me, I feel I have to do this. When I started planning exactly how I would kiss Evan goodbye, I knew I was in trouble. So here we go. Leaving. If I get this right, the kiss will be slow, tender, and lingering. If will be sweet and poignant, sexy and restrained. It will break my heart, and I will go anyway.

I jumped into Evan's well. I do not know how long it has been since I did that. I did not fall, nor did I walk. A riddle of a journey, not properly one thing or another. To enter a well is to surrender to it. To become flow, to move through space and time, not directed by conscious choice but carried in the embrace of all that is. The wizard acts by their own will. I don't know the term for one who agrees to be acted on in this way.

There is, it is my conclusion, no thinking goddess of the tides to watch over its actions and determine the force and direction of each flow. Instead, the flow is the total of everything within it, the sum of those intentions and actions. Hard to think about. Forces acting on bodies, spaces responding to those actions on a grand scale.

I can see it all. The dizzy, vast expanse of power. Power to do more than travel. Instead, the means to shape and bend all things in accordance with will – if the will is powerful enough to do the bending. The power to enter the flow of infinite possibility and choose a single reality, a single truth from amongst the many. And so when the magicians meet themselves, they must explode because two ultimate solitary irrefutable truths cannot exist in the same space.

I have tasted the water from the well. I have seen the magician's journey, with all of its many temptations. I am just too lazy to want to spend all my time deliberately handcrafting every aspect of my reality. It cannot be worth the effort. I cannot imagine wanting anything that much to be willing to put in the graft. Also, I think I would get bored with my own ideas and the total lack of surprises, and I think once you start the artisanal reality game, if you let up on the slightest detail it could all fly apart in messy ways. As a human being it looks like my idleness might well be my saving grace in all of this.

Currently, I have no idea where I am. There's breadth and depth beyond anything I had seen before. The enormity of the tides is too big for my little head, which has started to cause me some navigational issues. No red shoes to reclaim, no scope for saying 'there's no place like home' and clicking my way out, because there are lots of places, equally uneasily like home.

Water connects all things. In wells and channels, in the seductive rhythm of waves on beaches. In underground streams and intermittent springs, shifting wetlands, bogs and estuaries. Wherever there is water, there is magical possibility. Quicksand realities. Places that come and go as the tide turns. Water flowing through every living thing, making us a part of the tide; in it and of it. How often do people trade places with themselves, and neither party is any the wiser? How many people who seem mad or out of kilter are merely displaced, having surfaced in the wrong pool, somewhere not their own? How do you know, when you walk out of the sea and up a beach whether you have truly returned to the same shore? The water in us may carry us away at any moment.

I am learning how to float in the sea. I leave my few worldly possessions on the beach and I go into the water. When I come back from the sea, I read this book to try and determine what has changed, what is the same. I know I am not alone, that other forms of myself have forsaken the magician's path too and that we show up on each other's beaches, to write letters in journals with pens of perplexing size and design. I was here. You were here. If you read this and do not recall writing it, there will be something to learn.

I write cautious love letters to myself in the sand, and when I come back I cannot tell how far the sea has taken those words. We are learning. I cannot do this alone, I know that much. At the margins of place, we are learning how to float on the sea and how to return to the shore and how not to need to control where we finally wash in.

My heart is very full. My heart is very empty. I feel the tide. I feel the changes. There can be no going back.

I do not recognise the woman in the mirror. She is wild haired with her sun bleached locks, and tanned hide. This is a creature like sea glass, washed and worn down by the waves over uncountable lifetimes. I do not know this woman who has been polished down to the bone and yet somehow still has skin. I have never seen her before.

This beach is not deserted. There are public toilets up by the road, and in the toilets there are mirrors and in the mirrors are truths I can make no sense of. Children and sandcastles play at normality. A bag that is apparently mine has money in it for food, for sugar-laden rubbish and the brightly coloured traps of oblivious civilization. My soul is hungry for candyfloss. For the easy slide back into empty things. I've tasted too much depth. My mouth has almost forgotten how to eat. The sky is too bright, too loud.

The children are too blurred in their excitement. I feel too heavy on the land, too solid and apparent now I have left the water. I have surely become a sea creature. It would not surprise me if I grew a tail and fins. This no longer feels like my element.

There is a still point. A place where the tides of self are not turning. It lies beyond the noise of thought and history. Beyond the details. We are coming to this place of quiet together. I touch it for a few moments, and each time it is easier to find. As slippery as truth. So ephemeral. A pond that waits for the ripple. A door into something I cannot name. The farther I go, the less I understand, but I feel that is as it should be. There is no one who can show me the way now. Me, myself and I, we will have to find it between us.

I am not a better person for all of this. My flaws are writ large across my many instalments. Self involved, attention hungry, but afraid of doing anything that would get me noticed. Generally lacking in empathy. A slow broil of self-dislike – not as fierce as it once was, but self-slaughter on the grand scale may have had a cathartic influence. I note that a less self-obsessed person would probably have a hard time with all this multiple identity stuff. I note that my inadequacies keep me moving. They may be my superpowers. If I could think of something to want, I could so easily become dangerous. I have the capacity for ruthlessness but I lack application.

I keep asking 'what happens next?' I don't know. I am waiting for something to change. For meaning to surrender itself into my arms. I must go down to the sea again, to the lonely sea and the sky. Isn't that it? I think about primate life emerging from water to land, and whether I am reversing that process, and what I may become if that's the case. As though we could rewind everything at will.

I have seen many seas. Some are the blue jewels of childhood's imagined oceans. I have waded out into water dark with pollution. I have swum with the plastic and the floating bodies of dead fish. There is no room here for squeamishness. I must go down to the sea again, to the sun bleached bones of whales and the strangulation of shopping bags. I must bob with the oil-encrusted birds on this final voyage to extinction. We're far beyond having single albatrosses around our necks now. I must go down to the sea where the selkie maidens no longer swim, and the mermaids have forsaken their tales for the sake of shoddy romances. There are better seas to be lost in, but to go there would be to carry worlds of poison into the last pristine places. We learn how to be the boundaries. All of me, no longer just riding these tides, but beginning to steer them. A complicity across countless thresholds. We will not meet each other for power's sake. We will not let the dead seas keep pouring into the living ones.

We have already done so much damage. We who would be magicians, who made cracks and tears in reality just to eat other versions of ourselves. When two versions of self become one, we make reality a little smaller. We ourselves become like holes in existence. Great gaping holes through which power flows so readily. Do I understand it now? Or is this another layer of illusion? Will I wake up tomorrow and find that reason has ebbed away again in the night, leaving me on yet another damp beach, with my understanding in tatters and some unfamiliar sea creature invading my clothes? I could spend forever trying to learn the secrets of the universe, but I still wouldn't really know. Magic is knowing precisely when to act. I do not reliably know when to act, or what to do. I am not a magician and perhaps this is a good thing.

I washed up on an unfamiliar shore. I have come to the conclusion that it does not matter where you are or where you have previously been, it is simply in the nature of shores to be unfamiliar when the sea casts you onto them. And at the same time, they are all so much alike. Sand. Pebbles digging into me, forcing me to pay attention. Sea smells. Slippery things. Crunchy dead things to alarm the bare foot. Litter. Mouth full of salt, body feeling like I'd been ground to tiny smoothness. This book. Is it my book? It is now. Why is it here? A bag full of uncanny things waits for me. Mine and not mine. Here we go again.

I know what's happened. Other versions of me have beached across worlds this morning. We are the survivors of a quest that has never followed the regular questing rules. I think that for a while, we were truly all the same person – that we became the perfect, all seeing, world striding tide owning magician. We understood what it means, and we chose, individually and also together, not to continue with it. I think I/we have been further along the magician's path and then chosen to stop than anyone else ever has.

Now, we are all back in the respective lands that formed us, and we have to figure out what to do with this choice. I have to decide what to do. There's no pre-designed path to follow here. No map of the terrain.

I still don't think this is a beach I've been to before. Why I washed up here, I have no idea. I came up the beach into a grove of holly trees. As I approached, I could see how time has layered up here, much as the regular sea stacks up sand dunes. The circle of hollies is so ancient that they have become something more than a physical presence of trees. They are a well, a whirlpool. Slippery prickly underfoot, oddly familiar as a sensation.

It threw me back to the memory of years ago, to my kid self slithering helplessly down a hill coated in holly leaves. A whole other me, as distant and alien as any self I found in the sea. I have not eaten all of the different people inside me – some of them are ghosts of my history, floating in their own little time bubbles. What does that mean? Perhaps that to eat a contemporary moment of self in another world is only part of the deal. There could be far more layers to this issue of becoming all of my possible selves.

I don't know where he came from. I guess in some ways he'd simply always been here and I didn't notice at first. Sun kissed skin and eyes full of recognition. A spirit of place. A land god. I don't know what to call him. Them. He's hardly the only one.

"There hasn't been a magician here in a long time," he said, by way of an introduction. Are all land spirits guys? Are all magicians women? What is this thing with the sexual chemistry? Is it that those who wish to be magicians are just turned on by anything resembling power? I don't know. He didn't know either.

The sea taught me to stop fighting. I needed to find my way back into my body. Not that I need to justify anything I've done. I am not making excuses for the fierce and tender fucking that ensued. I feel guilty about it though. About the power play, and the long history of my own family using the land. I feel guilty about Evan but not in an unfaithful way. More the question of what I could ever do with him that would not feel like using him. This man of the land could not have been more different from my horny valley god. His skin was largely free from fur, like velvet and honey. His hair silky in my hands, his sweat a new sea on my skin. Holly leaves make an unkind bed, suitable only for masochists, but I just didn't care and it was good.

"Have you ever watched the spooring part of a mushroom grow?" he asked me, afterwards. As you do in post coital conversations. I haven't seen that happen, no.

"Have you watched a plant burst up through the soil?"

I thought about stop motion photography. "Bit phallic?"

"Same urge." He said. "Shoving life up into the sky, big as we can. Full on. Of course humans prefer to see the earth as something they can plough and screw. The ever open, always generous thighs of the mother goddess. They cut down all the trees, when they can."

"So it's more father earth than mother earth?" I asked.

"No. The land is itself. Gender is a creature thing. People like me, we're about energy. Different sorts of energy. You're just understanding that as male because that's what makes sense to you."

"In your case it's all about thrusting?"

"That's the one." He gave me a second demonstration of this magical principle. This sort of philosophical work demands dedication, and attention to detail.

We talked for a while there, on and off. He told me that people see energy as people – even magicians. Our little ape brains can't handle it any other way.

"There didn't used to be tides like this," he said. "It's because you can't cope with ambiguity, with things happening and not happening all at once. So your magicians try to straighten it all out, to make straight lines, straight history, single truth. You push all the stories so far apart that they come crashing down into each other."

I asked him what he meant by this.

"Death. The ends of worlds. Chaos. The wrong sort of chaos, the infertile sort. Everything all trying to happen in the same place and the same time. Then your magic folk will come along to untangle it, put up walls and fences. Mark the edges, make the rules."

"That's not a tide."

"No. People have made their false tides for too long. The real tide... it is not like this."

The very act of trying to make sense of reality has an impact in it. This reminds me of those experiments where having someone looking changes whether you get a wave or a particle. Not that I ever understood any of that physics stuff. A mass human-gazing on reality, a mass belief in one true way changes how things are. There's no room for a multi-storyed kind of truth here. In their own way, every single person is a magician crafting their own reality out of what they are prepared to see, and what they refuse to acknowledge. We've gone for too much consensus. For the first time in what feels like lifetimes, I no longer have any sense that it's my job to sort this all out. I am very tired. I want to go home and sleep.

I'm walking home. I know exactly where home is, I feel it as a pull in my guts, an inner compass. I imagine this is what it's like for migrating birds and wildebeest, only there are no crocodile infested rivers on my route. The movement is still taking some getting used to. I'm not entire in my body, it feels like an alien container. My feet are bare, but I'm not feeling the grounder properly. It's as though my body is at one end of a tube and all the thinking and feeling apparatus is at the other end. I suspect I'm just out of practice at being a land mammal. It's like eating, which I haven't done in a long while. I don't remember how to feel hungry. I assume either it will come back, or I'll turn out to be able to photosynthesise, or I'll just fade away and stop.

Have I changed into something other than human? It would be tidier and more efficient not to eat and shit at all, it's certainly making life easier at the moment. No distractions. Perhaps I am absorbing sunlight and will eventually turn into a giant pea plant. Then, when I explode I will be peas rather than little, squelchy bits of failed magician. I'd got so used to thinking that I was bound to explode in the end. It had become a familiar, if grim sort of destiny. It is odd no longer thinking that I know how I'm going to die. Funny how comforting things can seem just by being familiar. Even the prospect of being spread thinly over a wide area. Mostly explosion is a consequence of accident, while the successfully eaten appear to burn away. But sometimes eating begets explosions. The most explosive me to date achieved a radius of about twelve feet.

I will go home and make sure that my valley is a safe place that cannot be drowned by the tides. I will see what else can be done. What makes sense. What feels like the sort of person I want to be. These are the questions to keep asking – not only 'who am I?' but 'what is my trajectory?' Where will this take me and who will I be, and is that what I wanted?

I have been a waif and a stray. I have been the angry, unwanted second sister. I have been friend to crows, casual lover of many, soul mate of none. I have been a world striding magician killing myself for power and I have been a dream bourn by a wave. I'd like to pause for a while and be a softly middle aged creature, in love with the land. In love with the spirit of the land. I will make cakes and curtains, not because I want to be the kind of virtuous girl-prisoner Mother Holle was after. Not to please anyone else, but to do the simplest, most basic and essential things on my own terms. To put down roots for a few years (back we go to photosynthesis). Get to know the valley.

I am going back to Grandma's House. I will be the wide-eyed girl in the hood, but I will also be the woodswoman and the wolf, and I'll be crazy Granny as well in my own time.

Fifth verse (then repeat the chorus) Forty-Two

I keep the door locked, and there's a large, plainly printed, very readable 'closed' sign on it. Of course there are a lot of people who gaze through the windows. I assume some of them aspire to buying books, but I know that's not what most of them are looking for. When the light comes from the west at just the right angle in the late afternoon, I can see the man who is keeping vigil out there; the echo of another city. The closed sign does not cause these various people to give up hope, or to go away.

The whole place smells of books. Dusty, leather-bound books no one buys, not least because I never let anyone through the front door. 'Merryweathers' as Bookends has been unsubtly re-named, is not yet open for business, and probably never will be. It exists to ground Evan's story. I can give him that much, at any rate. Here we are, improvising wildly, waiting for things to happen, and making islands in the tide. It looks exactly like a bookshop – lots of shelves and books, just no customers. There's a little bell on the door which never tinkles because the door never opens to let any potential book buyers in. This is not about having a shop. This is about creating something people can believe in. It feels a tad manipulative to me, but that's what wizards do, and Merryweather is nothing if not a wizard.

Today, the bell on the locked door tinkled. The door that does not open, opened. A person walked in, ignoring the books and heading straight for me, bringing a wash of aching familiarity I could not place at first.

"Hello Katherine." A velvet voice, one to stroke a person's soul.

I stared blankly for a few seconds, feeling like a total idiot, unable to think or remember. "Do I know you?" Awful, pathetic, but at the same time, feeling that I did know, should know.

"It's been a while." This said with a wicked smile, playing the game of making me squirm.

Not many people call me Katherine.

"Oh, give me a clue then. How long?"

"Fourteen years, seven months and five days by my counting, but time's not the most reliable thing is it?"

I did the maths. I would have been twenty eight. I lived in several different places that year and I started moving about between worlds a well. I met a lot of people. Most of those people have only ever been a vague blur for me. I squinted at the person in my bookshop. A beautiful, androgynous face, weathered and softly lined, with deep dark eyes.

"Harri?"

They nodded. We stood there for a while, both of us lost for words.

"Photos afterwards, or at the very least, details," Evan said, breaking the spell. I hadn't even heard him come in. He nodded to me. Permission. Blessing. Pervert. He knows me too well.

"Partner?" Harri asked. "Are introductions appropriate?"

I found my voice. "This is Harri, who I last saw jumping into a faerie-tale well. This is Evan, whose longevity has enabled him to shag the vast majority of my ancestors."

"Ah," said Evan.

"Well then," said Harri.

Gloucester has changed a lot in the last few years. At first I tried to keep track of the intrusions as other Gloucesters pressed close together. The first of these that I observed was the overnight arrival of a pub called The Duke of Gloucester – a large, slightly sinister building that seldom has anyone going into it. Many of the changes have been smaller. There are more trees, more skin colours, more kinds of ears. I've stopped trying to track it, and find it ever harder to remember what was properly my Gloucester and what has just turned up.

Every couple of months or so, a carpet salesman shows up on Barton Street. Dodgy, second hand flying carpets that you have to barter for. On the plus side, car theft for joy riding is at an all time low. At the same time, the number of people accidentally on roofs they can't get down from without help, has increased considerably. By silent agreement, we are all undertaking to act as though nothing odd is going on, and that a night on the town in Gloucester always contained the risk of a stampeding elephant, or an act of spontaneous human combustion.

Because of course sometimes it goes wrong in the shifting multi-plated interlaced knockabout of the many Gloucesters. Sudden, violent combustions happen most weeks. Mostly we're (and by we I mean me) getting the pushing together to work, and the city stretches and expands to accommodate itself differently. We all get used to a less linear approach to space and time. By 'we' on this occasion, I mostly mean everyone else. I am not used to it, and the ease with which the people around me have taken it in their stride, apparently ignoring most of the upheavals, awes me.

I took Harri for coffee in the old part of town. A patisserie that used to open onto one of the four main roads. It's been less popular since a temple to some kind of tentacle Goddess popped up next door, and an intermittent circus started appearing outside. The Nightmouse Circus. Self-proclaimed sinister rodents who leer at you through the window if you're in the cafe eating cake. Harri loved them.

We tried to explain to each other where we have been all these years and what we've been doing. In the end, we both gave up and tortured the mice with badly made napkin puppets. Harri was all for checking out the circus, but I don't know where it goes, when it goes, and the mice seem profoundly untrustworthy.

It's funny, I've spent years thinking about all the things I would ask Harri if I ever got the chance. All the things I don't know and wanted to know. Who are they? Where did they come from and where did they go? What was that strange interlude with me all about? And of course if they came back I would want to ask them why they came back and how they found me and what it all meant.

Except I haven't asked a single one of those questions. I enjoyed the wondering. I realise that I don't want answers after all. Harri is a beautiful enigma. If I pushed too hard to extract details, it would be like those old collectors who pinned butterflies to boards. Yes, you end up with a solid thing you can keep and it looks exactly like a dead butterfly. However, it rather assumes that the body of the butterfly is the thing. An immobile butterfly is only part of a butterfly. The rest of it has always existed in the movement, in the flitting and landing on flowers, and catching the sun and all the other ever shifting details of butterflyness. That's Harri. Pin them down, and some of the most essential Harriness would be lost, and I don't want that.

All of the book bindings were blue this morning. I asked Evan what it means, but he claims not to know. It's his bookshop. He says its Merryweather's bookshop. I pointed out that as he made Merryweather up, the bookshop is his, and he ought to know what's going on in it. "I didn't make her up, I discovered her," he said. I keep telling him he can't make me be Merryweather, but here I am in this crazy shop and if Evan doesn't know what's going on, who does? What is this place? I though Evan set it up, but it turns out that he bought it, stock and all, from someone else. I asked who. "He was just a guy," Evan says. "It was a long time ago, I don't really remember. It was called Bookends then."

It's an old building. Some of the bits in the middle are all at funny angles with exposed beams and whatnot. I've seen it before – people add bits on to buildings, one generation after another. They can end up like Russian dolls, with the original property hidden from the outside, nesting in the middle. I know which bit I think is the middle. There are some very odd books in it – huge, leather-bound and impossible to read, I think they're in English, just an English so old and odd that I can't fathom it at all.

What if this was a magical building before Evan took it on? What if the person who put it all together was the real deal? What if Evan didn't entirely imagine Merryweather, but tapped into something in the history of the building? What if all of this stacks up, and has a certain energy to it because this is the real Merryweather's bookshop? Something is going on here, there is a magic inherent to the place and I am not the one creating it. If there is another wizard, perhaps historical in the mix, it raises the question of where the real Merryweather is (or whatever their name is/was). And what Evan's got himself into need considering, too. Is there a lingering presence of Merryweather here, somehow, that has influenced him? Am I just going round in circles?

I know I'm obsessing, but I can't stop trying to figure the Merryweather stuff out. That name has been with me for such a long time now, from my first crossings, really. It feels significant and I cannot ignore it. Perhaps, like Evan, I'm succumbing to something soaked into the walls here that make me want to go a Merryweathering.

Which leads me to a question. Can I do with time the sorts of things I can do with space? The idea of messing with time makes me nervous because I keep thinking about paradoxes. I also don't like the idea that if I move in time I can't change anything because everything is predestined and could only ever fall out in one way. That's worse than the risk of paradox. That's utter pointlessness to everything ever.

All the sci-fi I've ever read or watched seems to treat time and space as inter-related. Space and place, that's all very flexible and negotiable, and not very solid, at least in theory. I experience time in one direction, because that's mostly what people do. Is it the only way? Can I take the consequences to my poor little animal body and brain of messing about with this? I know as I write this that I'm writing it to talk myself into having a go.

Physical thresholds are easier places for making crossings between worlds. Wells, ruined arches, barrows... it's just easier for the body to accept it, I think. So working on that theory, moving through time would be easier in places that feel old. Some of the bookshop is very old. If I go right into the middle, into the oldest architecture – maybe the chimney in that section for extra threshold points, maybe I could stand there and give time a little prod and see what happens. If Merryweather existed, it may be a case of when, but perhaps I can go there.

He looked like my father. Exactly like my father did when I was a kid and would sometimes creep to the door of his studio to watch him painting. Not that I could ever see what he was doing, just his shoulders hunched over whatever tiny project he was working on. My father is not just a miniaturist, but a strictly non-representational artist as well. It bothered me as a child, it seemed like he was painting the sorts of things I should be painting and not the sorts of things a proper grown up should be painting.

This eerie father doppelganger was also doing non-representational art – in that it didn't look like physical reality, but it did definitely look like something. Maps of neural pathways, or illustrations of how magnetic fields intersect with deep sea currents, perhaps. Paintings of how a single human life is modified by the cycle of the seasons. I'm just guessing. The images felt important when I saw them and the act of his painting them seemed like something magical, sacred and not to be intruded upon. I've never felt this way about my parent, so take it as evidence that I met something other than him.

It was not like watching God paint the universe into being because I suspect that would be way more intimidating, but that's an idea it led me to.

When he noticed me, he smiled. Again, proof that this was not the father I grew up with. Then he held up a painting, in which he had painted my father painting a picture of me, and somehow I was painting the canvas he was painting on, and the room around him. It made me feel uneasy.

"You aren't my father," I said. Which I admit is not my best conversation opener to date.

"I am what your father wanted to be," he said, unhelpfully. I couldn't bring myself to ask what he meant. I am happy not to know.

"Is this your house?" I asked.

"Well yes."

"Why am I here?"

He smiled at me again, not unkindly. "Surely you are better placed to answer that than I am?"

"Are you Merryweather?" And why wasn't he bothered by my showing up like this?

He gestured across the room to a large, dark and slumbering cat.

"That's Merryweather?" I asked.

He confessed that indeed, the cat had that name.

"Is he a shapeshifter, or a wizard from another world?" I asked, desperately trying to make sense of things.

"No," said the painter. "As far as I know, he's just my cat. He snores a lot, and he farts loudly."

Merryweather opened a large, yellow eye and considered me. He said nothing with either end.

Here's my theory. The Dad-like man living somewhere in the past in the middle of the bookshop is a direct ancestor of mine, a wizard, and the source of the Merryweather myths. He has no reason to tell me the truth, after all, and if he's the source of Merryweather, he obviously has his reasons for the great Merryweather farce and this is all supposed to achieve something. How would I tell if I was forging my own destiny or playing out another wizard's strategy?

We were in the valley, Evan and I. Far enough in for it to feel otherworldly, close enough to the edge to still feel the tug of home.

"Do you know why I built my cottage where I did?" he asked.

It was one of those conversations I expect I'll remember perfectly for the rest of my life, but I'm going to write it down anyway, just to be on the safe side.

I said: "To stop people wandering in?"

"Yes, and no. Places like this shouldn't be cut off from people. There should be flow, but there isn't. I had to cut it off specifically to keep your lot out."

"My family?"

"Yes."

I feel responsible for this even though it's not my fault.

"I don't think my dad or my sister do this stuff. Am I the last one?"

"You are."

"Well, I'm never going to have kids, so once I'm dead, you can safely open it up again."

There was an expression on his face at that point, one I'd never seen before and could not read, but it gave me goose bumps.

"You'll live longer than most, mind," he said, not looking at me as he spoke. "You don't age as much when you spend time here. It's one of the reasons magicians want it. Immortality, and power."

"But unless a person stays here all the time, they age and die, right?"

"Right," he said. "Right."

"But you let me in," I said – in part just to change direction.

"You broke in," he said, finding a smile.

"Only the first time," I pointed out.

"I'll never forget the sight of you that night, coming down out of the valley, wet, filthy, half child, half woman, not yet a sorcerer but clearly heading that way. I looked at you and it struck me that you really were everything I was looking for."

"Pervert," I said.

He nodded, but said, "Mostly I was thinking about Merryweather."

The image of him, and his face on that night has always been with me. I knew he'd just lied to me. It wasn't recognition, or ambition, or seeing a dream come to life, it was regret, pure and simple. And I still don't know what he was regretting. So I said, "It was just love at first sight, admit it."

Evan laughed. "Far more cynical than that. A sense of your usefulness, and your potential to change things."

That felt a bit more like truth. Maybe not a whole truth.

Of course it was love at first sight for me, but I won't tell him that. I know how this works. I fall in love a lot. I do it wildly, fiercely, without reason or restraint. At least on the inside. That sort of thing cannot be returned or requited. It's too much. Too big. I love with everything I am, everything I have and when it becomes too much to bear, we move on. It's just that Evan and I are tied together in more complicated ways than usual.

The lodgers in my grandmother's cottage enjoy unexpected good fortune and terminate their contract early. This is because I need them to leave. I try not to pull on the delicate threads of reality too often, but it feels important and I trust that. I need to be back in the house.

It's funny how the underlying smell of the house – lavender and yesterday's baking – never changes, no matter who lives there, or how much dust and stale air there is. I remember being here as a kid, hoping for the discovery of a gothic manuscript or an ancient artefact, and finding nothing. A whole line of sorcerers could reasonably be expected to leave some kind of trace. I just didn't know what to look for – not a magic spoon, or a trapdoor like I'd expected, but the building itself, and the memories stored within the walls. My relationship with time and space has changed considerably of late. I know how to get inside the heart of a building.

I've made a few journeys into what I think of as the memory of the bookshop. Sometimes I see the man who is not my father, sometimes there are other people, making strange, luminous, unsettling forms of art that have all the logic of a dream to them. I wonder if I am seeing my ancestors. I still don't know. It is not the same as entering history and participating in it – that isn't available to me at the moment. It's more like a collective memory, a dream of what was that exists outside of time but parallel to it in some way. That's the best I've got for now. There is always a cat, and as far as I can make out, always the same cat – the one introduced to me as Merryweather. The cat does not talk to me, but I think it is expressing something by letting me see it like this. It wants me to be aware of it, and there are reasons for the other things I am being shown, as well. One of the reasons is quite possibly so that I could learn about the heart of buildings, and the memories of places. The way spaces and stories intersect, with time bent sidewise into the fabric of a place. I've stopped trying to rationalise this – neither time, space nor magic are especially rational things.

I go to Grandmother's house.

Geographically speaking, the middle of the house is the chimney. It could well be the oldest part of the building too, as that's often the case. So, I climbed into the fireplace. Sure enough, there were steps inside it, sooty but firm. I had a feeling they would be there. It's not just a matter of taking yourself into the older parts of a construction. I have to walk through time as well, and a staircase going up is not the easiest thing to turn into a route into the past. I focused on the old stone, the ancient soot stains. Crusted on shit from countless generations of chimney-adoring jackdaws. Time enough, it turned out.

It makes sense that a kitchen would be the very centre of a house like this one. Baking bread, the smell of laundry, a reminder of Mother Holle. A pile of steaming loaves on the kitchen table, immaculate white tablecloth, which spattered red when I tore the first loaf open. Inside the bread it was raw and bloody, like an unborn thing, and I did not feel inspired to eat it. You get into these things because you think it's going to be like in films and an Important Clue will reveal itself. No such luck. Just the kitchen downstairs, a bedroom upstairs, no one else about – if you don't count the blood loaves. So I went back to the chimney, and further back into the house's ideas about the past.

A darker, older cottage, no glass in the windows just wooden shutters. Laundry smells. Fresh loaves on a bare wooden table that caught the blood when I tested the bread. Just the same. No revelations, just slightly gruesome baking. Back and back I went. Table, blood loaf, no human presence. Back until there wasn't a cottage anymore, just the valley, empty of human presence.

Where the cottage had been, I found a tree. Twisting trunk before me, heavy branches laden with golden apples.

"And what sort of tree are you?" I asked it.

"I'm excellent," said the apple tree.

"I was wondering if you were one of those mythical, magical apple trees?"

"Well, obviously," said the tree. "You only have to look at the otherworldly sheen on my fruit to see that, and here I am, at an entrance to another world. How could I possibly be anything but enchanted?"

And there was a clue in the talking, as well.

"What happens if I eat one of your apples, assuming you let me?"

"Oh, help yourself. But you get what you get."

For a while, neither of us said anything, but an idea turned up and I am not honestly sure whether it was my idea or whether it came from the tree. I picked an apple and pocketed it. I took some time then just to be there, to smell and feel the valley as it had been before my family started making a nuisance of themselves. It wasn't as I had first thought it to be – not pristinely free of human activity. I could smell wood smoke, hear voices. There were people in the trees, they just weren't messing anything up.

"Important life lesson," said the tree. "People are natural too. People who forget that they are natural can be a bit of a problem."

I thanked it and left, because knowing what I needed to do next put a bit of a taint on hanging out and admiring the scenery. I don't know where the insight came from, but it was absolutely right. I am tempted to say that the answers were in my blood all along.

There wasn't a cottage in this oldest valley, so there wasn't a chimney, which made the process of retracing my steps challenging. I collected some larger stones that were lying around, gathered twigs and made a small fire in the improvised fireplace. Enough to be the beginning of the ancestral chimney. Enough to flag up to the ancestors yet to come that this would be the place to start. I'm not getting into the pre-destined argument again because it makes me miserable. I do not know if sorcerer time is the same as real time. And anyway, time is irrational.

I stepped into the fire, and into all the chimneys that would be, and started the long, slightly singed journey back.

In every kitchen, a table and on every table, I found the freshly baked blood loaves. An uneasy kind of magic, which felt familiar even though I couldn't figure out what it was for or how it worked. Bread is for eating. No matter what horror or intent is baked into it, bread is for eating and so I ate it. Every last loaf, with every last raw and bloody centre, in every single version of the cottage I could find.

I've had a lot of practice in the art of eating disgusting things. All those years spent eating vile versions of myself have given me quite a capacity, and a cast iron constitution. I can be sickened, and still keep going. But oh dear gods it was hard. No matter how sweet and tasty the outside of the loaves were, each one had the unborn centre, bloody, sometimes pulsing with uncanny life. Not quite alive, but certainly not dead. A profound wrongness, a history of wrongness.

I had plenty of time while I was eating to really think about what was going into my mouth. How had fresh blood got into something baked? Why wasn't the blood cooked solid? Who the hell makes that sort of thing anyway? My family, by the looks of it. These are my people, this is where I come from. What does that make me?

When I got back to the kitchen that had no loaves, I slumped down at the table and wept with relief. The knowledge of how to make the loaves was in the bread, and I had that inside of me, now, but not the reasoning behind it. A spell without a story is of limited use. That story had been passed one generation to the next, I could feel it, but no one had told it to me, and they should have done. Someone broke with tradition, and did not pass the knowledge down.

My guess is that it was my father, who may have been obliged to eat his own loaf at some point, and decided not to have me do it as well. He did not bake me a blood bread. All of his cold, weird distance I can forgive if he knew this and chose to protect me from it. I am not like the rest of them, and that's very likely thanks to him. I've become a different sort of wizard to my exploding ancestors, and it is almost certainly his rejection of tradition that gave me the chance to be as I am.

I feel lighter now, thinking that. But at the time, I mostly felt bloated, and sick to my soul. Then the pain started. The most hideous gut pain I have ever known and I felt sure I was going to die. Some sort of instinct took over and I ran out into the front garden, in the gloom, because it was just before dawn by then. I dropped my trousers, squatted and it all poured out of me. All the nasty shit of my family history, processed through my body, exploding out of my arse into the cool morning air because my body just couldn't hold it in any longer.

When it was over, I stood next to the huge pile, shaking, sore, crying. It didn't smell too bad. It already looked more like soil than shit and I watched it settle down into the earth beneath it, looking more innocent by the moment. Around me, the sun came up and the birds, who had been tweeting for a while, began to sing in earnest.

Then I remembered the apple, which had stayed safely in my trousers the whole time. I took it out and the dawn light glowed across its golden skin. The sheer beauty of it awed and humbled me.

I ate the apple, and it tasted of forgiveness. There was just one seed in the middle. I took that seed, and very carefully planted it into my ancestral shit pile, and lay down on the grass near it, and went to sleep.

I woke to the smell of bread baking. Warm sun. My sister in the kitchen, sounding cheerful. I went inside, asked what she was up to. Apparently I once listed her as my next of kin and the letting agents contact her every time the place is empty and I don't respond to them. Which has probably happened a lot, and I'd never thought about it. When it happens, she comes over and looks after things. It troubles me that I did not know this, but it reassures me to realise she does this as a free holiday and escape from my mother and not out of any desire to help me.

Looking at her in the cottage that morning I could see all the tangled threads of our maternal line wrapped around her throat and tugging at her hair. I was tempted to remove those binds from her, but there was no knowing what the consequences would be. Sudden change can be a massive shock to the system.

She took a loaf out of the oven, and I spontaneously threw up all over the floor.

So the house and my sister still exist. Whatever the implications of the things I've done (paradox, free will etc) I have not unmade us. We are still here, but something, certainly, has changed. I'm not sure what.

I do know I was away long enough to trigger my sister's arrival and that she did not see me sleeping in the garden.

Merryweather says, "Eaten your share of loaves and fishes?" It's the first time he's communicated verbally. I let it be known that indeed, I had.

"Magic is so often just a matter of what you can manage to eat. I ate an entire magician once, and it did me no good at all. Terrible indigestion, he kept reoccurring on me. Now I just focus my attention on the useful bits. Hearts, brains, spleen..."

"Spleens?" I couldn't resist asking, despite the implications for my own safety. I had to know.

"In my experience, often the most magical part of the body." He eyed me up in a way I found deeply disconcerting. "They taste best after they've exploded, of course." He commenced paw cleaning, then after gnawing on a couple of his toes, continued. "Throwing up what you don't personally need is the best way to read the entrails," he said, nonchalantly. "I wonder what yours would say?"

"Are you threatening me?" I asked, while trying not to sound threatened.

"I prefer to think of it as making polite conversation."

"I thought this was more than small talk."

"Did you think I was helping you? Let me be entirely honest for a moment. I will only help you in so far as it serves my purposes. I want this place open. It improves the hunting. Keep a comfortable home for me, and I won't trouble you."

"You'll trouble someone, though," I said.

I've never seen a cat shrug before. Merryweather shrugged. "If it's no one you like, what do you care? You don't care if a fox eats a pigeon, do you?

He had a fair point. "If I don't know what you're doing and it has no impact on me, I guess it can't be a problem," I said.

"That's the spirit," said Merryweather. "No eating anyone's friends and it's all peachy keen."

On reflection I'm glad I've never mentioned Merryweather to Evan. The truth would make him feel sad, I think. He gets sentimentally attached to all kinds of things, his own ideas especially. I may not make any more visits to the centre of the bookshop if I can avoid it – leave the cat to it. Not think too much about who his mice might be.

Today, every third book spine is green and we have a lot of books called "How to make Stuff out of Things." I feel that if a person knew how to do it, the bookshop itself could be read as a form of divination, and it would reveal a great deal. Worlds touch here, but do not collide. Something of a glorious multiverse reflects in the bindings and titles. Probably in the contents as well, but I can't always read the text. I don't know enough about what's happening in the worlds. I never feel like I know enough. How do you read a bookshop? Are books the entrails of civilizations? Where's the spleen? Merryweather is right and if I knew how to just eat the juicy bits out of the books, I would.

I feel, most of the time, like I'm wandering about in a fog. I'm not all here, but I have no idea where the rest of me is or what it might be doing. A bit like being in the sea, I suppose. I don't know what I've eaten. Yes, sure, on a metaphysical level the idea of letting go of the ancestral shit is all well and good. Except I've pulled something out of time, pulled it right through myself and into the now. If a cat chews a ball of string and eats it and later you try and pull the dangling end from its arse, you can pull all the intestines out. Entrails again, and some uneasy thoughts about what mine would say if examined.

I was in the sea for months, at least. When I came back, it took me weeks to learn how to eat and drink like a person again. I can jump into fires and travel through time. I need to stop treating this body as though it is some kind of normal, human body.

I go back to Merryweather and tell him to go ahead and read my entrails. He seems pleased. It hurts, obviously, and it is a bit weird looking down at them all as the cat rifles through my body cavity in search of clues. He kindly shows me what my spleen looks like. He licks it, and I remind him that I am not there to be snacked on. My blood runs freely down my legs and across the floor as my intestines run through his claws, and I do not die. When he is done looking, he folds them all carefully away inside me again, and I use a needle and thread to sew my stomach shut.

"Your body is going to keep surprising you," he says, between mouthfuls. He's licking up my blood, I am a snack after all.

"You can be the bookshop," he says.

This sounds to me like something you'd get on cheap noodle packaging. A dubious translation, meaning largely lost.

"You are tasty!" Noodle packaging again.

I'm looking for truth, revelation, epiphany. It seems like a lot of effort to have gone to for the sort of empty platitudes he's dishing out.

"You want to hear, but also you don't want to hear," he says.

"I want to hear. Tell me, I've spilled my guts, what did you make of it?"

He licks his lips, there is still some of my blood in the fur around his chin. "You've got the means to change things. Really change things. You can become whatever you want. This bookshop. The whole city. All of the Gloucesters. Probably the only limits are your courage and your imagination."

"Why would I want to become Gloucester? It's dirty and full of people and there's a sinister mouse circus in it."

"You might want to do it because that might be what it takes. You know things about threads and about tides, but what do you think those are, really?"

"I guess I don't know."

"Power. Energy. Life. Wizards get power hungry and they suck out too much energy from the worlds. It's like pulling threads out of a cloth. Do it for long enough, and you get holes. Your cloth falls apart. To make new threads, you have to put energy in. Life. Your life. You become the city, or the hill, or whatever, and you can change the shape of what's there. Restore it. Whatever you choose to be, you can change."

"It's not my job to fix everything."

The cat raised his paws defensively. "Hey, I'm just the message bearer. These are your entrails."

I hate binary choices. Yes or No. There's got to be something in between. Evan noticed my bright blue stitches and asked what I'd been up to. I couldn't face explaining things. To my shame, I fobbed him off with allusions to 'wizard stuff'. It doesn't seem like a good time to tell him about Merryweather, much less to try and discuss what Merryweather said. I'm not sure that I want anyone else to know this about me.

So I went to the sinister mouse circus. For the escapism. "Existential crisis guaranteed," said the Dormouse. Door Mouse. Whatever. "Personal unease, mild disaffection, the kind of apathy you can have before lunch without ruining your appetite entirely."

Inside the circus, it was dark. There were noises; some giggling, and shuffling sounds. I detected a lingering smell of sawdust and wee. Or popcorn. Hard to be sure. Uncomfortable wooden seats. Every now and then, someone played a single note on what sounded like a badly tuned triangle. I got up to leave, but there were no exit signs. I blundered about in the dark, banging into things. None of them felt like people but some of them complained anyway. I slipped in something and bashed my knee on something else and the stitches went in my stomach and I could feel the blood and entrails coming out.

The lights came up then, revealing a lone mouse in a pink tutu, wobbling on a unicycle, and me, doing a one woman impression of a zombie apocalypse. The actual people in the audience started screaming and running away – I guess they got their money's worth. The circus mice offered me thread, and a contract to work full time with them.

Mugged by Neo-Neolithics. It has been a day. I'd assumed they were from one of the other

Gloucesters, having seen a few of them from afar before now. Close up is a whole other experience. They smelled rank enough to seem authentic, but some of them were distinctly wearing fur fabric and those who had skins clearly didn't know much about skin preparation and even less about how to use flint tools.

They mugged me for my shopping. I tried telling them bread was exactly the thing people on paleo diets don't eat and that my processed cheese was certainly not going to do them any good. This is when I learned that they call themselves Neo-Neolithics.

"It's not the fucking paleo diet, right? It's not a dairy free, gluten free lifestyle."

"So, what is it then?" I asked, still clinging to my proto-lunch.

"Hunter gatherer, living off the land, off our wits. Fuck industry. Fuck work. Fuck capitalism. Fuck contemporary western civilization."

I admit to having had a hard time taking them seriously. "So you're what, foraging me?

"No, we're mugging you," one of them helpfully explained, and then they grabbed my bag and ran off with it, leaving a trail of moulting animal fur behind them.

"This is how the world ends," Harri said, when I told them what had happened. I'd been obliged to get chips instead and brought those safely back. I may have cheated a bit.

"Seen it before, on my travels. People latch onto an idea they think is going to save them. Next thing you know, they're sacrificing each other to a God they just invented, or convinced they've got to drink more, or less, or kill some other group of people."

"Or dress themselves in the skins of ineptly slaughtered animals?"

"It fits the pattern. It's about finding something to blame, and something to believe in."

I pointed out how silly and pointless the whole thing had seemed.

"Don't you get it?" Harri asked. "It's not about solving any actual problems. It's a make believe of having all the answers already so you don't really have to deal with the stuff that scares you."

With hindsight, I could wish I'd stopped them by force.

I am afraid that the people wearing togas might think they are Neo-Neolithics too, but don't have a very good grasp of history. I'm not sure what the people in the helmets are doing. There's been a massive outbreak of behaviour not normal for Gloucester. Harri says this is how it goes when worlds collide. They will go mad and set about killing each other. The high tides make people crazy. Collisions of realities, exploding magicians and sudden overlaps causing combustion are pretty minor threats at the moment compared to the very real risks of the things we are poised to do to ourselves, and each other. It has been worse other places, Harri says. Not all other places, but some. I keep thinking about what Merryweather said, and wondering if Merryweather was wrong. Or lying. I'm not sure what causes what. Places, tides, people, madness. I am not making any sudden decisions.

It looks to me like 'hunter gatherer lifestyle' in Gloucester means breaking windows and looting. It's been a long week. There seem to be ever more Dukes in The Duke of Gloucester. I feel like they're plotting something, but that may be irrational. Then we started getting the butt naked people in blue war paint, and I thought we'd got a Celtic re-enactment answer to Neo-Neolithics. But no. They really are from away, they speak a whole other language and have a wattle and daub encampment by the bridge at Over. They seem to be having their own private war with a bunch of ninja monk types who are camped out on the far side of Blackfriars. There wasn't a big apple orchard out there, previously, so I assume that came along with them. Both groups pass through the city like they don't know our version of it exists, which is creepy to watch.

The Neo-Neolithics don't seem to like this new development with the actually historical peoples moving in. The number of people taking most of their clothes off and trying to turn broom handles into spears increases by the day. This is not a good environment for books. The front few shelves nearest the windows have emptied of their own free will and I keep finding nervous book stacks trying to hide in corners of other rooms. I'm going to board up the windows and make the place unavailable while I think about things. If all of the books panic and try to run, it's going to be chaos in here.

The trouble is, I don't think people round here are going mad. I wish I thought they were, it would be easier to deal with. This is how people are when acting as part of a large, frightened group. I can't go out there and talk them down one at a time, there are too many of them. Yes, sure, I probably could take over a swathe of this reality by force of will and make them all behave, but what actual good would that do? It's only a temporary solution, depending on my ability to keep things up, and that's without getting into the freewill malarkey again. What's the point of developing god-like powers if you have to then use them to micromanage the lives of innumerable fools?

Most of the people running round in leopard print leotards and Argos rugs are enjoying themselves with all this chaos and mayhem. The drama of it. The group panic brings its own pleasures, by the looks of it. Each one of them is living out their own personal apocalypse fantasy and trying to bond with likeminded souls to make it really real. Better than reality TV. Better than computer games. Real fighting. Real death. Real going hungry. Your Game of Mad Max's Thunderdrome Thorn Throne Game Game. The dress rehearsals have been going on for years, and no one realised.

It could be worse. Someone in Birmingham has decided to try and set up the hunger games. I gather from the radio that someone in North Wales thinks we can fix everything if he just takes a bunch of hobbits to the top of Snowdon. I feel like everyone has been making their plans for quite some time, and I missed a memo.

Don't knock what you haven't tried, right? There's a rather musty zebra skin in one of the more Victorian corners of the inner bookshop. I was concerned it might crumble away to dust like something shifted through time in a H. Rider Haggard novel if I brought it out. It didn't, so I stripped off and used the spindly stripy legs to tie it in place. Almost decent and not likely to freeze to death.

"When I said I had a leather fetish, I was more thinking of trousers, to be honest," Evan said, with an over-enthusiastic approach to my stripy behind. When I said I wasn't wearing it for him he checked my forehead temperature, and asked if I'd been drinking. "When did this urge come upon you?" he asked.

"It's not an irrational impulse, it is a disguise for my carefully considered plan."

"I expect that's what they all say, at the start."

I can't always tell when he's teasing me. This was one of those.

Here are the results of my reconnaissance mission: At the moment it is safer being out on the streets of Gloucester in an antique zebra hide than it is in regular attire. Like most lifestylers, the other Neo-Neolithics are ok with anyone they think is 'one of them'. There are a lot of broken windows in the city. Most of the shops have been foraged to the point of emptiness and are now are barren wastelands as far as edible substances are concerned. Only twenty first century luxury goods are in reliable supply and no one wants those enough to steal them. They're far too last civilization.

The trouble with the Neo-Neolithics is they don't have the practical skills to back up their image. Fire building, after you've used all the stolen matches and firelighters, is a thing you need to do as a self-elected member of the Stone Age. You need to know what of the wild plant-matter you can eat. How to fish would be a useful insight. At least they're all still happy to accept that water comes out of taps. There are people dying of violence and starvation out there. They're doing this to themselves and apparently they can't see it.

The Dukes of Gloucester have fortified their inn. The Celts control the riverbank, and kill anyone who gets in their way. The ninja monks seem equally well organised, but the sinister mouse circus has packed up and moved on. There's a whole new tower at Westgate and a massive tree growing out of what used to be the Guildhall. I think there may be a giant kraken in the docks but didn't get a proper look.

There is, I admit, something liberating about running round wearing only a skin. Knowing I don't have to go back to my old life. The immediacy of starving or being killed all feels very real. More joyful than fearful. I think I'm starting to understand them. Out on the streets as a Neo-Neolithic, it's just life and death. No rules. No responsibilities. Eat dandelions and pigeons until you take a gamble on a pretty mushroom, and die. They have broken the cages and chains. Short, nasty and brutish as a lifestyle suddenly seems more appealing to a lot of people than a slow, beige office death. Blood replaces the bloodless. Time becomes precious and uncontrollable all at once. Be glorious. Be a half naked hero. Fight, fuck and do not fear tomorrow. Die from infected wounds because you lost a fight with a badger. It all raises a lot of questions about what civilisation is really for.

The tide is coming in hardest to Gloucester. I've been studying the news, what little of it there is, and putting out my own feelers. I've been thinking about what Evan said, about the valley. That's a shore, a place the tides come to. I've been back a few times just to feel it and get the flavour of it. Gloucester does not leave the same taste in the back of the mouth. Something else is happening here. It tastes like a tightly wound elastic band. It tastes like strain and old rubber.

I cheat a lot. Takeaway is easier to find when you have more space and time to play with, and I like takeaway. I met another me in a different chip shop. Still black and white half timbered, but a good deal more headroom. The guy at the counter kept calling me 'shorty' and the other me was probably twice my height. We approached each other carefully to avoid carnage.

"You're not from round here," the other me said, casually.

As this Gloucester seemed a lot saner than mine, I popped my food parcels home to the family and went back to talk to myself. Turned out that their Gloucester had Puritans, Born Again Atheists, a soup kitchen, and a soup dragon. The vast majority of the population had taken to putting colourful plastic buckets on their heads and pretending that they were playing a deep immersion virtual reality computer game.

Purely by chance, we ran into a third me who had crept into this Gloucester to pick up some coffee and bananas. Most of her Gloucester was on fire and the alien mothership was expected to turn up any day. She seemed sceptical about the odds of this coming to pass. We swapped notes. They'd been coming to the same conclusion as me – that something is specifically wrong with Gloucester that is more than the magician-messed intensity of a change in the tides. Something is inherently wrong with Gloucester – and while we all had a bit of a laugh about that, there's a deeper truth to it. A wrong that is too wrong.

We're all young in our craft, we've none of us had much access to older mages, but there are people we've all met versions of. We've all three of us encountered Evan – although we know he's a singularity. It seems I have encountered him most. We have all encountered Merryweather, but there is no knowing if that's a singularity or a multiplicity. None of our Merryweathers are the magician of legend, mine is the only cat, all of them seem a bit off in some way. We have gut feelings and no certainties. We've all been encouraged by our respective Merryweathers to become Gloucester, and none of us feel comfortable about it. We all have a Harri in our backgrounds – each a different tale of love, loss and longing. I find it hard to imagine there could be more than one Harri, and from the timing it looks to me like they've had time to work through us individually. Is it wrong of me to find that sexy?

We want to change what's happening. Not just soften the blows of impact, but get underneath the surface of this and understand the process. We're all wary about taking too much responsibility, but we're also all hungry to know.

During the conversation it struck each of us individually what particularly fine examples of ourselves we all were and how much better we were than the all the other versions of ourselves we'd eaten back when we were younger and did not know any better. We all said so. It was a heart warming experience and left me with the embryo of an idea and perhaps the makings of a cunning plan.

Here's what I'm thinking. The thing about magicians is that they are normally solitary. Even

Evan wasn't optimistic enough to spin wizardly co-operation into his Merryweather stories. I do wonder about his choice of name, though. I wonder if the cat gave him the name, or has moved into the story for its own convenience. Is there one Merryweather? Or many, playing with the name and the stories? Just because a talking cat with chronological displacement issues tells me I've got to become Gloucester to save all the worlds does not make this true. I don't trust the cat.

What would happen if multiple me took the advice to become Gloucester, when our individual Gloucesters are knocking into each other and seem intent on being just the one Gloucester? I have a feeling this would not go well for me/us. But what purpose does it serve? Not my purpose, I suspect. Not the purpose served by choosing to stay plural. It might even be a way of attacking my plurality. Am I being paranoid? Maybe. Am I right? Hard to tell. The implications are interesting.

This is just an idea, based on an understanding (which is not necessarily a complete understanding) of what a magician really is. I want to say that I'm unique, even though there are clearly a few of me knocking around out there. We're spanning the worlds. We're multiple magicians who have stopped not because we had to, but because we chose to. It would of course be better if we'd not eaten so many other versions between us. We have connections with each other, and with places, and I think we could use that to reduce the violence in the tides. I've been doing bits and pieces on my own to try and cushion things. Small, persuasive magic, just to keep the bumps minimal. I like to think of myself as a re-usable airbag for the great reality car crash.

I've been working towards this idea for a while now, and recent timely conversations have put a few more details in place. If we were all a teensy bit magical, but everywhere, my cunning plan would be even more likely to work. That's irony for you. Now ask what the benefits would be of keeping the tides violent, and ask what that would serve, and a distinct picture starts to emerge. I'm thinking obliquely because if I think too directly I may draw attention. The ether is a delicate place at the best of times. I want to leave a trail in case it doesn't work and someone follows after – I expect Evan would go through my things and read this, so I'm writing it for you right now. I have no idea what you will make of my ramblings, but there are suggestions here and you've probably got time to ponder the subtext, Evan.

There are all kinds of things a magician can feed on. Fear, violence, conflict and destruction are all on the list. It's just a case of how much you can eat, and of what flavour. If a person were very good at feeding on conflict and collision, a person could get a lot of mileage out of what's happening in Gloucester right now.

I think it likely that all the other surviving mes are coming to this same conclusion. I know at least two others are thinking the same way, but that's likely not enough. I will pick a place and time, and by magic, it will be the right place and time. Now I need to find a concept that frames it all and makes it all work. Not too dictatorial. Not telling people who and how and where to be, more giving them a better start at sorting it out for themselves. I need to make more airbags for the reality car crash. I need to dissipate the energy like a parachute jumper does when hitting the ground. Keep something in motion and you can avoid all the metaphorical broken ankles. What can I move? Where can I move the energy to?

The Ninja monks are building what looks like siege towers. This inclines me to think they're going after The Dukes of Gloucester. The inn became a castle at some point when I wasn't looking. Some of the Neo-Neolithics have evidently switched period allegiance and become mediaeval cannon fodder instead. The Celtic settlement at Over seems a tad unnerved by the elephants grazing on the Forest side of the river. These are big, hairy elephants, but not actually mammoths I think. I have no idea what their presence means, but I enjoy watching them. Whatever is living in the docks has reduced every last boat to small pieces of debris, even the metal ones. There are rumours of a unicorn in the woods around Robinswood Hill and tales that Dursley has been over-run with flesh eating zombies. I'm not sure how anyone would tell the difference on that last one.

Funnily enough, the answer was there all along. That's probably the case with most ideas. Truly new things are pretty rare, after all. I found a whole stack of map books in the bathroom – evidently they're still nervous about the possible antics of humans. I guess some of these books are old enough to remember the last time this sort of tidal crash happened. You think of books as remembering what is in them, not what's happened to them. But then, until recently I hadn't thought books would split into groups of approximately similar subject matter and look for places to hide, either. They don't leave tracks in the dust, so I assume they can fly when no one is watching them.

The big, ancient, chained-down antiquarian books are increasingly excited, or nervous. I can hear them rattling said chains and banging against the doors at all hours of the day and night. I don't dare go in there. Evan says they've always been a bit temperamental! Deeply affected by the positions of the stars and planets, he said.

Filing books round here is a truly inexact science. It doesn't help that the bindings spontaneously change or perhaps the books themselves disappear, exchanging their positions with other titles in other magical bookshops. There's no way of knowing. Whatever they do, they do it when I'm not here, or when I'm looking the other way. There must be other versions of this shop so the idea that books move between shops doesn't seem unreasonable. The shop exists in the Gloucesters and is more stable than not, for suitable values of 'stable'. It tends to be bigger on the inside than on the outside, it is full of time, and shifting words. Book sorting is an approximate business because the vast majority of these books could be listed in so many ways – with spine colour being by no means the least relevant consideration. I think they like being sorted by colour.

On the plus side, if a book doesn't like where it's been put, it moves. We tried to sort out the plant books this morning, and the gardening books took umbrage at the process and went off on their own to found a little colony in a pile on top of the architecture books.

People are not so very different to books. We're all full of facts, theories and stories too. Red on the inside, as dear old Clive Barker would say. Books of blood, us. So mostly it's a case of figuring out the genres. The comedies and tragedies, the action adventures and the cosy mysteries. Are you a none-too-graphic murder solved by a middle aged tea drinker and her dog? Or are you a sex jazz apocalypse with a dash of political commentary?

Tricky, but not impossible.

When I first envisioned making a means for people to sort themselves out, I pictured it as high drama. Me on a windswept hilltop, arms wide, clothes and hair billowing around me theatrically. Dark clouds boiling overhead. Ominous thunder. Channelling the tidal energy into safe movement. The parachute collapses, the jumper hits the ground and rolls, no ankles are broken. The sense of countless other versions of myself on many hills through many worlds. Lightning flashes, and dances around my hands.

The trouble is that for all the visual impact I'd get, a hill and a thunderstorm has no natural resonance with my intentions, so that's a non-starter already. I am not parachute jumping, however much I might like the metaphor.

Aside from myself, I've not done a lot of killing. I don't think the blood loaves really count. I've never set out to consciously try and kill something that wasn't me before. I may not be quite as evil as I thought I was because I feel pretty uneasy about this. I am however, plenty evil enough to go through with it. I don't want to say too much, or think too much because it's a delicate plan depending more on uncanny insight than is morally comfortable when planning a murder. When it comes down to it, I trust my uncanny insight. If I don't come back, you'll just have to learn to live with the not knowing. Sorry Evan, if you're reading this. I really hope I'm coming back.

How to change everything. How to save everyone from themselves – or at least give them an option and commit just the one murder so that the imaginary parachute jumpers do not splinter their bones so badly. I thought I should leave a record in case any future wizard types turn out to need some pointers when in a similar fix. If you get another likely looking candidate, Evan, pass them what I have. I know a lot of this sounds like bollocks, but it might help a future wizard to at least make new and different mistakes. The idea of a similar fix seems unlikely but we are talking multiple worlds here, who knows what multi-faceted ways things might play out in. It is at least safe to think and write about recent events now, where before it most assuredly was not.

Dear Evan, posterity and struggling future wizards, here is a rundown of what I've been up to, what I know, and my speculations.

People can be enabled to self-sort by genre, as though they are books. It just calls for opening up a multiplicity of ways between places so that anyone who wants to can, during the brief time slot, float off to a bookcase/reality that better suits them. I know it's tempting to sort people out, to want to organise them but it is better to let people do it for themselves and just facilitate the process.

The movement of sorting dissipates excess energy. The sorting process itself creates new threads in the weave of reality. It's not exactly patching the holes magician moths have chewed, but new threads help with the stability of things a bit, as far as I can make out.

The deepest heart of Merryweather's Bookshop is a place of power and a natural hub of tidal activity. It is not impacted by the tides, making it an idea point from which to work with tidal motion. Make sure you know who is living in it and controlling it, and watch out for other islands, because they too will be places of power. I knew as soon as I thought of this that the cat would likely prove hostile to any action on my part. Places of power attract hungry predators. It is worth being suspicious of anything residing at an obvious hub.

To create distraction I focused all my attention on singing little songs to myself all the time I was walking my way into the heart of the building. Any entity occupying a place of power should be assumed to be capable of picking up on the intentions of a being or beings moving towards it. Seeming nonchalant down to your last cell and hair follicle is thus vital to survival and success. Down all the twisty, turny ways I went, where walls and time grow thick and dusty.

Usually the heart of the bookshop is a room, sometimes with a moment from the past playing out in it. Not today. Merryweather knew I was coming, and although the cat was not fully prepared for me, I knew he knew that something was afoot. He chose to make this obvious – or perhaps could not control the consequences of certain emotional states. When I arrived, the heart of the bookshop was truly a heart – bloody, beating, deafening. There was no sign of the cat.

These are the things that have become clear to me during the process, although I'd suspected some of them for a while: Merryweather the magician and the bookshop had been one and the same for some time. The clue was the suggestion that I could become Gloucester if I wanted. It made sense of how Merryweather has been able to act not only on Evan, but on the denizens of other worlds who come into contact with the building.

We fought. I want to give you guidance and insight here because this was an unusual fight, and any future wizard facing the same would benefit from insights. I'm finding it hard to think of any words that do it justice. We did battle with the rhythms of hearts and the power each of us holds in our blood. Time became a weapon that either of us could utilise. He wielded the weight of the past like a giant hammer that could have crushed me entirely. I went in already armed with the keen edges of future possibility, ideal for slicing and needling. We fought long, and we fought for no time at all. Merryweather's key advantage lay in him also being the building. He cut off the air, re-imagined the gravity, pulled and pushed at the laws of physics to knock me about and disorder my body and mind.

He must, surely, have been one of the most powerful sorcerers who ever lived. I would guess he had long since successfully eaten all other versions of himself. By holding time at the heart of the bookshop, he had gained a form of immortality. It looked like a dull and sterile sort of life, though. The nature of Merryweather's power also created his greatest weakness. I find that's often the way of it. There was only one of him. There are rather a lot of me. After a while what I'd hoped would happen evidently was occurring – Merryweather had to divide his attention between various versions of me who had all come to the same conclusion and headed in. Dealing with multiple me took a toll on his massive singularity.

We couldn't just kill him – that was something I'd not entirely planned for but became evident once the battle was in full swing. I didn't want to destroy the building, I needed the hub nature of it, but to triumph over the sorcerer cat without wrecking the location he had become? This is not the kind of thing you get pointers on in any of the grimoires. What I've come up with is not conventional magical theory, but it is tried and tested.

The method for defeating the magician without losing the usefulness of the occupied building: Merryweather talked to me a lot on previous encounters about eating power, so every time he seemed distracted, I took a lick of the walls. They tasted of heart, certainly. I toyed with the idea of trying to find his spleen, his self-confessed magical centre. I doubt I could find one on an organ diagram – inside a giant cat-wizard-building seems out of my league. If you know where a spleen might be, it's something to consider.

Things I learned from the heart: It tasted of distraction and poor concentration, too much time, of boredom and greed, and green pepper and leaf litter and raw beef. I kept licking. It felt weirdly intimate as a thing to be doing, and honestly, a bit perverted. I could make out the threads of different lives, the many flavours of Merryweather all tangled up together in this huge mess of time and power. A taste of near-explosion. The taste of a man still eating himself. Lick by lick, each flavour became distinctly recognisable from the others. A buttery sort of

Merryweather. A piquant Merryweather. A cardboard one. There were a lot of flavours.

It took a lot of time and persistent licking, which will not be to everyone's tastes. (Ha!) I disentangled the Merryeathers with my tongue. It's about getting into all the holes and cracks, opening them up. I guess you work with what you've got. Appetite is my superpower, that, and licking. Other people craft, incant, gesticulate. I chew. I break things down to their essence.

The number of Merryweathers I chewed loose certainly supports the theory that he'd entirely eaten himself. There were far more of them than there were of me, but once they were pulled apart, they were small, confused, tired things. They were used to being one entity and many hadn't thought of themselves as separate entities for hundreds of years, at a guess. As a consequence they couldn't organise as individuals to put up any real resistance. I could feel the other versions of myself, sometimes at the edges of my personal reality bubble. Sometimes I caught glimpses of them. We took the many Merryweathers and pulled apart the threads of them, and with this raw material we fashioned doors and made a bookshop that was open and that straddled all the worlds, and in which people could be sorted by genre. Of course that was just the start, but it gives you an idea of what can be done, and how.

We wove the worlds and the spaces between worlds, the ways of leaving and the ways of arriving. We wove the lines from past to future , the parallel threads of different selves, with room inside for all the lives that never were and all the choices never explored.

For a while there, I could see it all – an exquisite, multi-dimensional rug of staggering complexity. All that vastness, made of nothing more than the tiny threads of individual lives, weaving together endlessly in the day to day knots of living and being. Fault lines and broken threads became visible, too – the hollow gaps where magicians had made holes, like invading hordes of moth caterpillars gnawing on the tapestry of existence. If too many moths get in the woolly hats, everything falls apart – I speak from grim experience here. Where new magicians nibbled away at the fabric, we pulled them loose from the threads and threw them away. I do not know what happened to them or where 'away' is.

It takes all of a person's possible selves to be the magician with the power to control the tides and all the known worlds. Only it turns out that you can do that as a team, not as a lonely victor with a long history of self-annihilation. It's just a case of reaching across the gaps. If we hadn't spent that time in the sea we would not have had the knowledge or connections to do this. I feel that the tide chose us, chose me in all my many forms to be its healer. I'm ok with that idea now. I think I'd felt it, in an unconscious way for most of my life, and resented the sense of pressure. It doesn't seem so intimidating now that I really get the scale of the thing, and the limitless possibility that is me. That is any of us, I guess. The more room we have for our other selves, the better. I've tried to leave plenty of room in the fabric so that we can dream each other, remember ourselves bigger and wilder than one body can encompass.

Reality is a pattern woven on a loom whose frame is consciousness and whose weft is time. There are natural places of fold and overlap, and naturally occurring gaps. Take out the magician's chew damage and the natural rhythm of those gaps and passing points becomes more obvious. I'm not sure when I stopped thinking about tides and started thinking like threads, but it's like the whole business with light as wave or particle. It is a woven tapestry, and it is also an ebbing, flowing sea, and it is made of many layers. Take whichever metaphor works best in the moment, because they're only stories to wrap around a truth too big to contemplate.

I can see the threads that weave between the fabrics of different worlds. My threads. Evan. Harri is an interesting maker of connections, far more travelled and influencing than I had ever realised before. There are others I've not met yet, but whose threading lives add richness rather than doing damage. There are forms of magic, it relieves me to see, that are not about power and consumption.

I have seen the tides, and the natural ebb and flow of them. And I could see the distortion where the deliberate use of power act on them, the pull of Merryweather's rent like a black hole, sucking everything out of shape and towards one spot. I could see Evan tangled through time and around this place, caught in the web of it. Drawn to it for the very reasons that made it so damaging. A well meaning desire to fix things, twisted so that those good intentions served to protect the very problem.

To reach out as a magician and touch a thread is to change it. The slightest tremor in the fabric of reality can have vast consequences. I could not untangle Evan from Merryweather without creating yet more changes. Given what I'd already done to Merryweather, I could hardly leave Evan entangled in that mess. It is possible to know everything, but the act of knowing everything defines the kind of outcomes you get. To know all possible outcomes for Evan would be to destroy him – to rob him of free will. It is only because reality does not allow itself to know everything that we have room for ourselves. But to untangle him blindly, without seeing – that wasn't without risk either.

And so, with all the love I have in my soul, and my eyes firmly closed against the consequences, I untangled him and released his thread to find its own way into the great weave. I will have to live with the consequences, whatever those turn out to be.

There has only ever been the one Evan. There are many versions of me, but I am the single version to have become his lover. I'm fairly sure there is also only the one Harri, although having seen the threads, it is clear this one Harri has known many versions of me. I wonder about the drops of inspiration and knowledge Harri sprinkled over my life(lives). I would not be the me that I am without Harri's influence.

The army of me did not initially set out to repair the Merryweather rent. Instead, we made use of the damage to create an opening across the worlds, just for a little while. Then the sorting. The pied piper dance across space, flying through the rifts and rents to the place your soul belongs. Person by person, to sort yourself by the genres you would choose to live. Swapping lives and souls back and forth between possible realities, in a search for harmony and balance. Because your souls have been displaced so many times by these over-violent tides. So many of you were not where you should have been. I learned on my travels that to be gone too long from your rightful place is to be unhinged, alienated. So deep, and so widespread was the unhinging that it too was gnawing into the fabric of existence.

As we held the ways open, I saw a thing that I had not previously been able to imagine. I saw the threads of lives weaving back and forth between worlds, creating dimensions of tapestry where before there had been only void. I took the beauty of this process as a sign of truth. I saw how gently the tides rippled over these new threads, like friendly stream currents over water weeds.

I did not become Gloucester. I became everything. The loom, the threads and the tides. Only for a while. It is too much to live in. No one can know that much for long without becoming harmful. What I saw with Evan – that I would destroy him by knowing his future – is true of everything. Too much knowing takes away free will. I will have to go back there now and then to check for the nibbling damage from rapacious magicians, but I can live with that and so, I think, can the rest of reality.

I could have chosen to stay in that state of power. I could become deity in this curious tangle of life. I do not think these worlds need an all present, all knowing, utterly powerful Goddess. I do not want to know all things. I do not want the responsibility. You can't have free will if someone else has undertaken to know everything. I'll be the laundry lady of the multiverse instead. I'll go in and pick magician caterpillars out of the woolly hats of existence when things need spring cleaning.

I wonder if this is what happened to the Gods of human history. There are so many myths and stories of times when Gods were around and busy. Do Gods grow up? Do they look around and realise that if they are omnipotent and omniscient, no one else gets to live their own life? Is that why there seem to be no Gods now? Will there be new ones, eventually, to go through the whole process again? Was Merryweather a God, of sorts? And of course I don't have these answers because I've chosen not to look too closely, and I have to get along by living with the questions and the ambiguity of not really knowing.

Traditionally, the adventure ends when you go back home after the big dramatic thing has happened. As though big dramatic things are only toys and we must put them down in order to live the proper, ordinary shape of our lives. My life seems to get more improper at every turn. From the outside, it could be said that I have a smallish, female-ish, middle-aged-ish sort of body. On the inside, I am worlds within worlds. It mostly feels like what's inside is too big for this thin layer of skin to contain, yet somehow, here it all is, realities and entrails in their proper places. Skin generally on the outside, wet bits in the middle.

I have a theory. I always have theories. I am an almost entirely theoretical life form some days. My theory in this case is that each flavour of me shaped the specific flavour of its world in the great soul re-shelving experiment. In this metaphor, I am the bookshelf and the genre label. I'm not sure what we call this particular me-world-genre. Nothing tidy. Well meaning but fundamentally a bit twisted. Gothic,

Lovecraftian magical realism capable of both tenderness and extreme violence.

The sinister mouse circus is back, right outside the Patisserie. There is, without any shadow of a doubt, some kind of giant octopus in the docks. Quite a lot of the newer buildings have gone from the city. The castle is full of tiny dragons and the local unicorn is a pervert. The Dukes of Gloucester is an inn again and on Thursday nights there are very exotic dancers. Half of the population are now living in huts on the flood meadows. Not a good strategy - clue is in the name, people. No sign of the ninja monks, but quite a lot of people are going around with brightly coloured buckets on their heads, presumably pretending to be involved in an incredibly high tech virtual reality game. Furry ears are 'in'. This, by the looks of it, is the Gloucester I deserve. I guess I can live with that.

Evan wasn't here when I returned. He's not in the valley either. I'm not sure where he is, or quite what I've done to him. The bookshop continues to be a place books migrate to, and people, and others migrate though. Some of us are just meant to keep moving. Some of us will need a while to figure out where we fit. I'm not sure which category I fall into right now, but I'm okay with that. I do not know what happens next. Turn the page when ready, consider the next chapter. I have — at least for the short term — chosen to step back, to be a smallish, human-ish, female-ish and to do something small in a humanish sort of way. The epic adventures aren't anyone's real job, are they? Or perhaps it's just better for all of us when that's the case. The thread of my life is the real job, and that doesn't stop just because

I've done the big things. What do you do when you feel like you've done the thing you were supposed to do? What happens after that?

I say I'm okay with it. I say I can go back, but there is no 'back' - not after where I've been. What I've been. I'm afraid of using the words that make most sense here. Afraid that to name it, on top of everything else is to tie me to this terrifying story of what I've become.

Sometimes, I can treat it like a mad dream, and then the day to day stuff is tolerable. I potter round the bookshop, watching the spines, waiting for Evan, talking to Harri, who is my only comfort in all of this. I can't face going into the middle of the building, or into time. I know Merryweather has gone, I can feel the absence, but I can't face getting in there to see how things look now. Pure cowardice, but there we go.

The city is settling down. While I know what I did, and why that rethreading of reality with the lives of people has stabilised things, it's hard to go out there on my two feet and look at the relatively modest forms of madness and say 'I made this.' Because that has consequences. Owning it is uneasy territory. I made this. I became part of something that could make this. I became unlike every other living thing that wanders these streets, and I feel painfully separate, distant, lost.

The thing about unlocking your true potential, is that you can be bigger than you feel comfortable with. I could do anything. I really, seriously could do anything I set my mind on, and in face of that, I've spent a lot of days doing nothing. Not daring to do anything at all. In case I do too much. In case I am too much. I am afraid of myself, and of what I have become or am becoming.

Gods.

You see, gods are fine as some sort of abstract notion. But when it starts to look like a realistic career choice, you start seeing the real horror of it. The horror of that much power and responsibility. The terror of being able to choose anything and being totally and utterly responsible for all possible consequences of that choice. This is how you end up living/hiding in the middle of a bookshop trying to nudge your food into coming towards you, because you are too afraid to be what you have become.

Here in the middle of a bookshop, afraid to go out, afraid to talk to anyone, I can see myself turning into Merryweather after all, and not in the way Evan intended. Now, there's a man who must know something about matters of power and responsibility, but I don't know where he is to go there and talk to him. I probably could know where he is, I could probably be there in a flash, and I don't want to handle it that way. I don't want the consequences.

Harri says to be patient, make no sudden moves, give it time. Harri knows everything that I fear, and is not afraid of me, which is comforting. But at the same time, I know they are waiting for me to act.

Series Six, because we keep milking it despite having done the big plot arc: Forty-Nine

Based on the year of my birth in relation to the current year, it seems fair to claim that I am just shy of my half-century. It does not strike me as a very useful measure of anything. I came back to this valley what feels like a lifetime ago. What I found when I first returned here was a place empty of human development. A large, friendly apple tree grows where my grandmother's house once stood. Each autumn the tree produces a bountiful crop of golden fruits that taste of life, hope and dreams, and never seem to rot. The birds love them and we share the abundance. The songs at dawn and sunset are extraordinary.

There is no cottage where I remember that Evan's cottage used to stand. There is no hedge that I could have climbed through as a teen, and no garden that I might have wandered in as a young woman. Just the wildness of the valley. A history erased. My history, and of course not just mine. Other people lived here, too. Other lives have been changed. I do not know what happened here or exactly when, and I have mixed feelings about it. No one comes here now.

I have made a small wattle and daub hut with a thatched roof. I cheated considerably by asking the various raw materials for their help. Being a Neo-

Neolithic has not come easily to me, and it wasn't an intentional direction on my part. It's just that I've been trying to find simpler, gentler ways of doing things, and this is what happened as a consequence. I can't think of anything I want more.

I have water fresh from the valley to drink and I have apples to eat and birds for company. Sometimes an otherworldly white hind or giant boar passes though, but they don't bother me and I don't bother them. I have become a hermit of sorts, living with the ghosts of my past and the consequences of my actions. And while it may not have been entirely the outcome I was hoping for, I'm able to accept it. I did a decent enough job of things, I did what needed doing.

I've made a shrine by the well, where the spring bubbles up that I once jumped into. It's not an act of religious dedication, more by way of an invitation. Healing is a process, not a sudden, single act of transformation, and the fabric of reality here has been eaten away at by numerous magicians over a very long time. The small wonders will come back now that it's safe, but it may take them a while. I am just signalling the change to them, and changing the dressings on the wounds. I am still bleeding every month or so. I bring my blood to the shrine, and apples. I make people and creatures out of twigs, and bring them along too. The birds leave feathers. We dream the land back into itself.

Being here, it is my teenage self I feel closest to. Lost, hungry, wide eyed, ignorant, innocent, aching with self-pity. The memory of her is oddly comforting to me. She feels the more real of the two of us.

I have a re-occurring dream that I am pregnant with Evan. He's growing inside me, beard and all. I am too old and too celibate these days to be pregnant with anything much. The blood I produce can hardly represent any actual fertility on my part. I limit my productive ambitions to growing potatoes and catching fish. Mostly I cheat at that, too. I sing the potatoes to harvest and I sing fish into my bucket and they are all far more obliging than I deserve.

In spring I watch the lower pools for frog and toad spawn, and the skies for returning swallows. I wait for the first leaves to unfurl, and I eat all manner of wild leaves, fresh from the plant and tasting of green. I do not have to eat much at all – I've never gone back to needing a normal diet since my time in the sea, but nibbling keeps me grounded. Food from the earth, to hold my barely-real body more firmly against this soil. I could stop eating and float away into the sky, I feel sure, but I'm not convinced it would be worth it.

Being a hermit is just a phase for me, I expect. I can't imagine what comes after it, but perhaps that's as it should be. It's all too big – the way light catches dew on a leaf. Wind sounding in the branches. I do not think I could bear much more in terms of details. I feel too much as it is. The soil is so very alive. I've turned into a tree and can only do things at a tree's speed. Sun and rain caress me. I am in love with the fungi in the soil. Our sharing is sensuous and eternal.

Summer, and I'm ripening, and full and my mind runs with the deer over the rocks, and sometimes I think I am the deer, and sometimes I am the rocks, and sometimes I am a watching tree whose bark they may stop to nibble. There are days like today when the sun is on my skin and my hands are in my mind enough that I can hold pen and paper, and pull words out of my head and remember my monkey origins.

Most of the time I am drunk on heat and pollen, lazy with the hum of bees and oblivious to myself.

There are a great many stories about people who see too much and then run wild in the forest for years while they recover from the overload. I remember these stories now, and I think I am one of the people who went too far, dared too much. Seasons turn, and have turned again, and much of the past seems like a hazy dream now. I could remember more clearly if I wanted to, but I do not want it. I want the smallest things. Ant on a bending grass leaf. Thistledown. The sheen of a snail's path across the rocks.

I hear stories from the branches and the earthworms. Relics of great truths are buried under layers of leaf mould and send new shoots up into my body. Everything around me has its kin and there are days when I think the loneliness will kill me. I do not need another human being to complete me. I am whole within myself. I have played at love and love affairs enough times – there is no answer in romance for me, there never was. The peace I crave, the communion I yearn for is more than any human could give me.

And yet at night I dream that I am pregnant, and growing ever rounder to accommodate the man/child within me. When I wake my heart is a broken stone that the dawn birds have to sing back into living wholeness for me.

There is a particular magic to autumn, when the winds blow up the length of the valley, carrying the leaves with them. It is all about the shape of the land, and the way the wind lifts as it passes through here. The leaves rise, a dark snowstorm defying gravity to race up above the trees that parented them. It is an uncanny sight. An enchanted, impossible gift from the land. The old is swept away, but given this final moment of strange glory. I watch the leaves wash upwards on their own secret tide, rising above the valley and disappearing into the landscape beyond, or at least so it seems from here.

I have not crossed the threshold into the otherness of the deeper valley. I only go so far as the well and my shrine. For all the years I have been here, I have felt no urge to go further. I have thought this was my choice, or perhaps the valley's preference, but either way the well is far enough and I leave the greater mysteries to themselves.

My dream body swells. My waking body slows and grows heavy. Time leans on me. I find it harder to tell between waking and sleeping. Is there any real difference? Could such a difference matter in the slightest?

There will not be a winter this year. Not for me. The leaves will fall, and the colours fade, and I will fade also. I know this in my bones.

For many years now I have made a point of not knowing what is coming, because knowing limits the options and takes away free will. Winter is coming, and I have chosen to know what happens next in my story, and by writing it down I will fix it in place and make it true. I think this act of writing my future will be my final spell. It goes like this...

I will make a bread oven out of stones and flour from grass seeds and crushed acorns. I will summon the wild yeast, fetch water from the spring and make bread. I will put some of my own blood into the bread. I will take an apple from the tree. When I pass the well as I leave, I will take water from there in my bucket and with the water, the apple and the bread about my person, I will walk into the valley. I will walk for as far as I am able to go. As far as feet and path will take me. I will find a place amongst the trees, where it is soft and sheltered, and I will put the bread, the apple and the bucket of water down very carefully. I know who and what I am. I know who and what you are and I write to enchant the threads into taking shape for me. Weave true, weave firm.

I will lie down on the forest floor. The day will be warm and gentle, the sky will be clear. In the otherworldly forests of the valley I will find that my dreaming body is in truth my real body. I will open my thighs for you, let what blood and pain come as is needed. I will open my body for you and you will journey through me, out of dreaming and into this valley that is part of your soul. You will come into this world as your full grown self, as you always were and always will be. Your birth is the healing of this land, and the future will be in your hands, not mine.

You will wash away the process of your birth with the water from the well. You will eat the apple, and go forth into the world.

I know what should happen at this point. You leave, and the life blood ebbs from me and the flesh rots from my bones and I return to the valley in my own way. A circle is completed. But still, I think we can have more time than this. I think you will recognise me, and stay with me for a little while. There will be chance to talk, to share something of who we have been to each other. Not a stark ending for me, but one full of warmth and relief. An autumn leaf rising high on the wind before returning to the soil that has nourished it. I do not know what you will say to me when the time comes, Evan. I will not look. I will not destroy your free will through knowing too much. I will not craft the future too tightly. I leave this spell loose and open and grant you the right to choose your own words when the time comes. I write for us a day and a night. I write for us more than was intended. This is my last spell. It is time to make the bread.

Part One: Seven

This is what she first remembers, which is not to say that it happened this way. She does not entirely trust memory, and with good reason. Her seventh birthday party, held at her grandmother's house, which is odd because she can't recall ever having visited there before. It isn't really a party because there are no other children – it's just her and Isobel, who is sulking. Katy doesn't care about any of these details because for once she's the centre of attention. Her grandmother keeps calling her 'Poppet' and there is so much cake that she's at risk of making herself sick. And there are party hats. Lots of different hats in all kinds of shapes and sizes, and no one today is going to tell her that she must quickly make up her mind and settle for just one of them. She plays with the hats, tries them on for size, experiments with combinations of multiple hats, and goes back for another slice of cake.

On the other side of the kitchen door, her father and grandmother have a row about something. It would hardly be a credible childhood memory if there weren't adults shouting in the background somewhere. This is one of her few happy childhood memories, and it has all the more pathos for not being as true as she wants it to be.

It is not that she is experiencing the surely-I-am-dying sensation of having eaten far too much cake in far too short a time. She really is dying. She knows what is happening. She does not want to know, but with the knowledge comes the memory of a whole other seventh birthday. It surfaces in her mind, the evil fairy no one wanted to invite to the party, the one who will spoil everything but cannot be denied. The evil fairy points out to her that this is her oldest childhood memory. Seven is rather late in life by most people's standards for recollection. She is sitting at the table in her grandmother's kitchen. Her father is there. Just the three of them, and the warm smell of freshly baked bread.

Only the past, and not the present. Only the past, but so real that she cannot think about herself in the abstract any more. She must stop being safely 'she' and work out how to be me again. Some new me, or an old one, it doesn't seem to matter. A me in the ancestral kitchen, with the smell of bread.

"It's taken some explaining," my father says. "Paperwork's been a nightmare."

"But you sorted it all out." This is not a question from my grandmother.

He concurs that he had. They do not elaborate on what any of this means.

"Felicity is finding it all very hard to take."

"That's not surprising. Your wife finds everything unbearably difficult at the best of times. She's utterly wet. I have no idea what possessed you to marry her."

My father shrugs. "It seemed like a good idea at the time." He points at me. "Will this one do?"

Granny makes an open handed gesture that I cannot translate. "Too early to say. I'll need some time."

My father looks tired. "She's lasted longer than the others."

"It's a good sign. None of mine made it beyond a few weeks."

"Why are you still doing this?" my father asks.

"It will work one day. A child of yours perhaps, or a child of Isobel's."

He glowers. "I really can't see me persuading Isobel to take up this kind of ... baking."

Granny sniffs. "Well, best hope this is the one, then."

He leaves me with her. I have made nothing of their conversation.

"Let's go for a little walk, poppet," Granny says.

I put on my coat. We go a little way together, to the door of another cottage where Granny has a muted conversation with a man I've not seen before. The real present washes over the vivid past. This is Evan. This is the first time I've seen him. He takes me by the hand and I walk with him. I am placid. Nothing seems strange to me. He doesn't talk, he just sits down on a bench after a while, and stares at me for the longest time. His eyes are sad. He nods slowly.

"Sorry about this," he says. And I know he really is very sorry about everything and most especially, he is sorry about me.

"Everything's broken," he says. He puts a hand to his temple, as though he is in pain. "I didn't know it would be like this." He takes my small, soft, child hand in his big one again. "I will tell you the whole truth, and then you have to choose, okay?"

I nod, even though I don't understand. An older me, who is also here in this moment knows that asking child me to choose in this situation is totally unfair. It is not a real choice, just a way for him to reduce his guilt.

"Afterwards, if you choose to live, you'll forget all about this conversation."

I don't know why I'm remembering it now, or in such an immediate way as though I am living it for the first time. It is as though I am dreaming, and I think perhaps I am having this strange dream because I am dying and because these lost events are a key part of why I am dying. I just go with it.

"It goes like this, little one. You come from a long line of people who wanted to be powerful. Each one of those people who wanted to be powerful has tried to create a special, magical child. I suppose the short explanation is, they think this magical child will allow them to control even greater forces. They're a greedy, selfish bunch. You are the third child your father has helped to make this way. He's not got much magic in him, but your grandmother promises him ever greater fame and fortune if he does what she wants, and so he keeps helping her, even though he doesn't much like it. She's too old now to make a blood child of her own. She made a dozen or so, back when she could, but none of them lived for very long."

"What happened to them?" I ask.

"They didn't really want to live, or to be what they were. They just died. Your father's other blood children were the same."

"Why didn't they want to live?"

"Because they didn't like the idea."

"Why?"

"Because I had this conversation with them, too, and told them what they were."

"Why?"

"Because I can't use a life that hasn't consented. But, I've never seen a blood child like you before. You are the real thing. You are magic, and they weren't."

"I want to know everything." Even at that age, I am hungry, one way or another.

"The blood child is a magical tradition passed down through your family. They have believed, for many generations that they could become incredibly powerful if they made the perfect magical child."

"By making me?"

"That's the one."

"Why? Why did they believe that?"

"Because a long time ago, I told them it would work."

"Why?"

"Because I dreamed about it, and my dreams are always true." He sighs, and then he continues.

My older, watching self knows I am hearing a confession. How much truth there is in it, is a whole other question.

"I was a youth, a long time ago, and I did not change. I'm not sure when I started getting older, or why – although I have my suspicions. I had a dream, a long time ago that if I did not find someone to rebirth me, I would grow old and eventually die, and the land here would grow barren and everything on it and in it would die too."

"That would be very sad." My child self is entirely sympathetic. My adult self knows that death is part of the deal, and wonders at the implications of cheating in this way.

"The dream I had showed me how to make the person who would make me young again. The person who could heal the land, and heal me, and put everything right. Your family aren't a nice bunch, but I let them stay here on the condition that they would help me make the blood child."

This does not sit perfectly alongside other things he has told me at other times, about my family's relationship with the valley. My child self knows nothing of this is just trying to make sense of things.

"So, I'm not a proper person, then?"

"You are entirely yourself, as real as anything else. You come from your family, just not in quite the same way that most children do. You were made to help me, but you don't have to. You can choose to be who you like, and you can choose what to do and how to live this life you have. At every turn, you will be free to choose."

"And what am I supposed to do?"

"You have to grow up, that's the first job."

"That sounds okay."

He touches my cheek with the palm of his hand. I can see everything in his face. Child me and adult me slide into alignment. There is need and longing, fear, grief, responsibility. There is shame, too. This is a small life to sacrifice for the sake of the land, but looking that small life in the eyes isn't so easy for him, even though he's planned this moment for a long time. My small life is what we're talking about here. Me-as-child understands that part of it now. He is telling me the truth. I am not a natural child. I am something of a changeling, foisted on my mother, unwelcome, uneasy. It would be too much to ask of anyone that they give unconditional love to a thing made from blood and bread, baked into only a semblance of humanity. I can forgive them for being unequal to the task. I can forgive them for making me, this life has held more than enough to make up for the cost of it.

I see this moment, and I see how it sits within a greater web of time and intention. I see the many threads that bind Evan to Merryweather. I see the mesh made by his having bought the bookshop and by his telling of Merryweather stories. He is trying to change things, to save what he loves most. To be the force of balance that he is supposed to be. I'm not sure why he thinks he is supposed to be a force for balance, but he does, and that shapes his actions. I wonder if anyone ever sat him down and told him that he had a choice.

This man, this being of magic who has made so much trouble in my life, who has perhaps made my life, is not a god. He does not know everything, and that's good news because it keeps all our options open. He makes mistakes, which is inevitable for those who are not gods. He is too generous by nature. He is unable to avoid loving the very thing he has set himself up to use and destroy.

I see how Merryweather feeds on him. I wonder where the first dream of the blood child came from, and what Merryweather is to my family. I wonder who set up whom, really. Who was using whom. Who made the rules of the game and who played along to their detriment. I see Evan aging and I see life slowly leached out of the valley. I see otherworlds.

I see myself. A thousand, thousand versions of myself. Blood child and natural child. People who are distinctly me and yet do not emerge from the same stories or ancestral lines. It is not simply a case of multiple selves playing out the alternatives in parallel worlds. It is all more subtle and more complex than that. It is not where we started from that makes us, on some deeper level, one and the same. It is also a question of the choices we made and the dreams we carried within us. This is what Merryweather did not understand and thus did not plan for. It was too big for him after all.

Other versions of myself, other people who have chosen to be me will find their own ways forward, with or without my specific manifestation in the mix. There's some comfort in that thought. I realise that am the only blood child to have ever survived this long, but even as a created thing I have lived a life real enough to form patterns of sympathy that connect me with other lives.

There are other ways to become a magician. You can dream your other selves rather than eating them.

There is blood in my mouth. Blood and bread. I remember exactly who and what I have eaten along the way.

An Interval: In which we step outside time to attend to certain necessities

Arguably I've died on a number of occasions now, or done things that should have killed me if this was any sort of normal body. Bleeding to death is just another round, a new possibility. It may or may not have long lasting consequences. But what is the alternative to dying? Life is all well and good when there's something you want to do with it. I'm just not sure anymore. I have done too much, seen and felt too much and I am weary. Oblivion looks like respite. I am far more afraid to carry on than I am to stop.

"I knew this would happen."

Harri's voice clarifies a number of points. I am still capable of processing sound even though I can feel nothing and am in darkness. I still exist in time, and what exists of me is recognisable.

"Which bit did you know would happen?" I ask. Partly to establish that I can fashion sound. Partly because I want to make sure that Harri doesn't know too much.

I imagine I can hear Harri smiling.

"That you'd back yourself into some kind of awkward corner, being heroic and suicidal all at the same time."

"I'm pretty sure I didn't choose this," I point out.

"I was more talking about the dying," Harri says. "You won't let Evan save you, so there's nothing really he can do although he has been trying."

I think about this. "He set me up all along to die this way. No one could birth him and hope to survive. He must have known that, or at least guessed it was a risk." I don't feel angry with him. I probably should but it would take far too much effort. "Where are we, and how are you talking to me?" I ask.

"You're exactly where you were, barely conscious. I'm inside your head. I would have thought that was obvious."

"So I'm imagining this?"

"No."

"How are you inside my head?"

"Magic. You're procrastinating, which is inherently pointless. I know you, Kathleen. Katherine The Great. Probably better than anyone else ever has. I know why you're lying here, waiting to die, refusing to be helped."

"Well, I don't know what's going on, so don't assume you have everything figured out. This is my head, I'm in charge."

"Okay then, here's what I have. This is in essence what you always do. Every version of you I've ever known. You have to keep your options open, you can't be tied to being one thing, one kind of person. It's why your relationships don't work out – you sabotage them so that they can't define you. Otherwise someone might decide you were straight, or a lesbian, or bi, or pansexual or gender fluid or transgender... I've known a lot of you. You know perfectly well that Evan can pull you out of this, but you're afraid that if he does, that will define you. Life after that will be narrowed down in some ways.

You've been pregnant with him. You're his mother, his lover, his friend. He also helped in the making of you, it's about as tangled, pervy and messy as things can get, but somehow you manage to be afraid that if he rescues you, it'll be hetronormative and you'll have been pinned down. That would be a loss of self, and you'd rather die whole than go back and let him reduce you by defining who you are in some way."

I wonder at this point if I've given my unconscious mind Harri's voice so that it can talk to me. Harri is in many ways everything I've ever wanted to be. A fluid and shifting person who can stop shifting any time they feel like it. A wanderer and adventurer who can settle down whenever they like. Both the most unfaithful and profoundly loyal person I have ever known.

Having given me time to think, Harri starts lecturing again. "Evan is a simple, earthy creature by nature. Full of lust, life and wilderness. You love him, but it's not enough."

"I'm always too hungry," I admit.

"But is that worth dying for?"

"Yes, I guess. Being me is worth dying for."

"Is it worth living for?"

"You make it sound so simple," I grumble.

"What if it is? What if you just have to dream up a better way out of this? You can't be bored with life already, surely? There's so much of it you haven't explored yet."

"I don't know."

"How about I rescue you? I could. I know how to do it. I can put you back together, give you a firm kick up your charmingly sexy butt and leave you to make the rest up as you go along. Not a tidy completion that leaves you feeling like you have to settle down and knit socks. Something that invites you to be your own, wild, free, directionless self. You still get to shag Evan, but you don't have to feel like he owns you."

"I love you, Harri."

"I know you do, babe. That's why I've rocked up to save you from your own daft ideas."

"Thanks."

"Hey, no big deal."

I can definitely feel Harri smiling.

"You know it's okay to love guys, don't you? It doesn't make you any less the many shaded pervert darling that you are. You don't have to go all tame. He doesn't want that from you."

"I guess."

More warmth from Harri.

"He's shagged more than half your ancestors for centuries, had a hand in your making and been re-born from your body. I really think that for most people, shagging the person who has been both your father and your child is off the scale measures of deviancy. I'm just mentioning this in case you hadn't thought about it properly."

"You're a star, you know that?"

"I know."

Section whatever: who's counting anyway?

One of the issues to consider with God-like powers, is the question of when to stop. There is no doubt that at some point you do have to stop. The trajectory here is obvious. You fix or change things that bother you, and then you fix things that are a little bit bigger, and when it's clear you can do that, you escalate just a bit more. Before you know it you are busy removing toxins from the soil and clearing plastic from the sea. You breathe life back into dying species. Eventually you get really carried away and take clay (because that's traditional) and make life forms from it, and you are totally impressed with yourself.

Maybe some of the things you make are a bit wonky. Maybe some aren't as symmetrical as you'd intended, and maybe they don't all play nicely, but this is what evolution is for.

But here's the fundamental philosophical problem with it all. Everything that exists is capable of will and intention. Every action which you tell yourself is about sorting things out, is also an act of forcing change. The more you use your God-like powers, the less consent there is. You tell yourself the ends justify the means. Fixing things starts to look like weeding a flower bed, or selecting out the sheep from amongst the goats. You start feeling entitled to wipe out whatever displeases you. Rules are made – your rules, based on your whims and preferences.

You are of course a jealous God – I don't think it's possible to be anything else. You don't want anything or anyone usurping your power, or paying more attention to someone other than you. It is not difficult to alert the sentient beings to your rules. Some of them will follow your rules, and make sure others follow the rules as well. Sooner or later the followers get all excited and start inventing rules on your behalf, and as you are a jealous God, you will be tempted to punish them for this. They may interpret this as meaning they need to really go after the people who are not following the rules they invented on your behalf. It gets messy.

Your followers worship you, and there is enough mortal ego bullshit still inside your divinely powerful soul for this to be addictive. Love me. Praise me. Fear me. Worship me. We all know the routine.

When you can do anything. When the only limit is your imagination, and your imagination is vast, 'what happens next?' becomes a rather serious sort of question.

What happens to Gods? Some of them, when they get too big and too powerful, are killed. Often they are dismembered by their own children, who will use the severed parts to make a new world, and set a whole new cycle of overblown godhood in motion. Gods like these have their tales and their seasons. They rise and fall, and the ones who don't find some sustainable way to keep doing that, the ones who get ideas about being the only one true God anyone will ever need for all time... those Gods are eventually torn limb from limb. It's the only way to stop them.

There are also, clearly, Gods who choose to stop. Absent parents to their creations, who choose to bugger off and not know everything so that what they have made can live on its own terms. I suspect being a God is much like being a wizard in that to accumulate that much personal power, you can't start out as the nicest of creatures. You have to be hungry, unreasonable and demanding. No truly ethical person goes the whole hog and becomes a deity. And so being ethical isn't what gets you there – you only have to look at old pantheons to know this. Godhood is a power grab. But, like anyone else, a God can wake up to the responsibilities and moral complexities of the job. You can start to question your right to micromanage lives. You can step back. Many do, although plenty of them leave a lot of trouble in their wake as they go.

I want to make less obvious mistakes than these, but it isn't easy.

When life and time are your playthings, how do you stop? When you can make things happen according to your will, how do you step away from that? How do you re-allow all that is to form its own opinions and make its own choices? Perhaps you go and hide in a valley and pretend you are not who you really are. Perhaps you try and go back to an ordinary life, promising that you won't cheat too often and take short-cuts that rob others of their free will. There are no active and ethical Gods. Just having that much power concentrated in one place unbalances things so that ethical options cease to exist. It is too much. I ran away to the valley because I had become a bloated, impossible thing. I could not live with myself as I was. I think Merryweather was working on being a God, and I did not want to follow where that path led.

It turns out that my beloved Harri is not afraid of Gods, nor much impressed by unthinkable power. Perhaps to Harri, the unthinkable has always been perfectly thinkable, and thus none of this is a big deal. My dear and generous friend, who has waited through all my wandering and hermiting and weirdness, and is somehow, magically still here. More than I could ever have deserved. I am grateful, and humbled, and awed.

Harri points out that there are always multiple options, never just the one. Seldom is it as simple as a binary choice if you take the time to look at things properly. The only limits on what I can do are my imagination and my willingness to act upon it. My real problem, it now seems, is that I am getting bogged down in the obvious ways of doing things.

I am not obliged to hang myself from a world tree or nail myself to anything in order to move on. I do not need to get my insights written down in a big book for posterity. Happily I'm not daft enough to think that the testament of Kathleen, failed sorcerer, part time saviour of worlds and slightly reluctant God of eating what is otherwise unacceptable and shitting out a better future, is going to catch on. This is not the handbook for easy solutions. I know that I have no desire to be worshipped and am on the whole rather glad that my efforts worked well enough to go largely unnoticed. I did not set out to be a deity, God only knows how I got into this state...

Harri says I should dream big, and dream wild and take my time over it. "Dream with your whole heart. Dream something fantastic that you can give as a gift to yourself. Find what you most want and be led by your hunger for it. Be bold." These are good words.

I have my suspicions about Harri, who always seems to be a step ahead of the game, dancing nimbly through all eventualities. Harri whose journey threads are part of what has held the many worlds in balance. I don't know, and I will neither ask nor look. But I rather think, that someone who had taken the ethical decision to stop playing God, but who remained interested in life, could very easily look a lot like Harri. Even if I'm wrong, it's good to have a role model at a time like this.

For some time now, I have tried to exist on a scale that makes no real sense to me. For all that I've been through, I still feel like a small mammal, descended from other small mammals. Just because we can expand to levels of unthinkable consciousness, doesn't necessarily mean we'll like it there. There is beauty in self containment and in being small enough to fit into a bigger picture. I want a life that is more inhabitable.

To forget would be to let parts of me die, to lose possibilities. As Harri pointed out, I'm not good at that. I want to hold on to everything that I might be, and this is how I get to the jealous part of the God role. Of course Gods die to themselves all the time, but I believe mostly they do so with a view to becoming more powerful afterwards, not less so. It's the big question, isn't it? Stay whole and be all that I possibly can be, or sacrifice some of that to be something that can have a life, rather than myriad uninhabitable possibilities.

And alongside that I must ask what gift I would give to myself. What is the best thing I could possibly imagine?

I have been a larger being than I knew how to bear. I have deliberately stripped myself back to the barest essentials of existing. One breath to the next, one sunrise to another, living small with the blades of grass and individual leaves. I have been a macrocosm and a microcosm because I could not remember how to live on a more human scale. I am a magician and occasional deity (which I think of as being kindred to the occasional table), not a physicist. I do not have to be either atoms or galaxies. I can live at the scale my human body expects to live at.

I have a body, and that body connects to the world. My feet upon the ground. The air in my lungs. My hands, able to touch. Lips of precisely the right size and shape for kissing other lips. I can smell the life of the soil, and the life in the skin. I can taste the air, the dew, the leaves. I can inhabit this shape, and gift this shape to anyone who wants to interact with it. Tree and dragonfly, sky and stream. Affectionate hands and open hearts. Person-shaped is not just a matter of shape and scale, it is about how this shaped is recognised by the fingers that touch it, the arms that open to it.

I remember.

The Exciting Movie Franchise Re-Boot: Twenty-One

My therapist says that journaling will help me create a private healing space for myself. I'm a bit of a mystery to all of us, but that's ok, they say. There are a lot of mysteries in the world and mysteries make life richer and more interesting.

So, here's what we know about me. I have no problem wielding a pen. My name is Kathleen Sylvia West. I have no living family members that anyone's been able to trace. I just surfaced a few weeks ago after being in a coma for a couple of years. While I was out, there was a period of total chaos and anarchy which is why records are in short supply. The best guess anyone has is that I suffered an injury or accident during that period and was lucky enough to be hospitalised and cared for. No one expected me to wake up, but with no next of kin to approve switching off the machines, I was accidentally given enough time to recover. Here I am. How or why I returned to consciousness we may never know, and I've been advised not to dwell on it.

I can remember nothing at all of my life before I woke up. I have no idea what I'm missing in not remembering, but I expect it makes me different from people who have history. I'm going to focus on going forward rather than trying to claw back what I've lost. It seems better that way.

It's curious though, because while I have nothing about who I am and where I come from, I can remember how to do all sorts of things. I know how to write, how to dance and how to bake bread. I can talk and think clearly, I am told. There are all sorts of things I don't understand, but that could be because they've changed while I was comatose. The question of who I am, and the follow up question of how I should live, are things I'm working on alongside getting strength back into my muscles.

My therapist tells me that I will discover who I am by watching what it is that I do. One choice at a time, I will solve this riddle. That feels exciting to me, so that in itself is something to know about who I am. The unknown excites me, and I am not afraid of it. I am happy to take things as they come, although keen to get started and a bit frustrated by the limitations of my body right now.

According to what little paperwork I have, I am twenty one. There's nothing to tell me where I have been or where I came from. The years between the registering of my birth, and now, are empty space. Twenty one is thus an empty number and feels meaningless to me. My therapist tells me it is possible that some or all of my memory will eventually return, but there are no guarantees. The probability seems to be that I will get something patchy. What this means is that I am given the freedom to invent myself as I go along.

Other known facts: I own a small, cheerful cottage in a pretty, wooded valley. There's a gorgeous apple tree in the garden. Seeing it brings back no memories at all. I've been living here for two days, and I feel like

I should remember, that my body being in this place should remember, but there's nothing. I know I can take as long as I need to do whatever I need to do. I have enough money to be blessed with all the time I might want or need to decide who I am and what I'm going to do. I like how this feels. Given my age I do not think I have earned this money. It is a gift – of fate, of luck, an accident of my birth – wherever it came from I am fortunate, and must not lose sight of that. It is easy to imagine a different story in which I woke up from my coma with nothing to my name, nowhere to go, and no way to fend for myself.

The clothes I own all seem very plain and simple. They surprise me, I look at them and I do not think they are the clothes I would choose. When I am feeling more settled, I will have to find better ones. Clearly me after coma is not the same as me before coma. I don't think these clothes suit me at all. Also, I think it would be nice to own a few hats.

Fact: I know how to drive, I am allowed to drive and I own a tiny car that is totally powered by my own wee. So I have to save up bottles of it for journeys. Something about it being powered by my wee cheers me enormously. I live a long way from shops, but there are apples on the tree at the moment, even out of season, and I don't think I need to eat a lot.

There is only one other cottage in the valley. It's further in, and appears to be made of moss-covered stones. It looks ancient. I don't remember my neighbour – of course – and we've not spoken yet. I saw him on my first day here. He's a bit older than me, I think. Hard to say how old he is, I don't know how to judge. He looks a bit wild and weathered – a good match for the cottage. He smiled and waved like he knew me, which I suppose he does. He may be able to help me piece together something to go into the empty space that is my memory. I expect there will be other people who have memories of me. That's going to be interesting.

I felt something when I saw him. Not like remembering, just a feeling. A really big feeling, intense and I don't know what to call it. My heart tells me that this man was important to me, before. I guess I'll just have to start from scratch and see what happens. I hope it's not too odd for him, me being back and yet not being me – or probably not the person I was before. The doorway to my past is closed, but I've peeked through the window by looking at things that were once mine, so I know I have changed.

It's all going to take time, my therapist tells me. I have to be gentle with myself. I think my therapist is a really good person and someone I can trust to guide me through all of this. They have a little consultation place in Gloucester, tucked in between a cauldron shop and a trendy Neo-Neolithic lunch bar. I am to go over every week, in my wee-powered car, and just talk about things. They're always helpful – they are the first person I remember seeing after I woke up in the hospital and they've helped me with everything. I am aware that in this too, I have been truly fortunate.

I may have a bit of a crush on them. Harri is gorgeous as well as being really kind to me. I expect they get that a lot with clients. Of course I'm not going to be a client forever, but as Harri says – one day at a time and no rushing.

Fin

Acknowledgements

I stole things off all sorts of people when putting this story together. Hopefully at this stage it isn't obvious what was me, and what I borrowed from Adam and Becca and Paul – with varying degrees of their knowing what I was doing. There's also the issue of the person I accidentally wrote before I met them, because that happens to me far too often, but there we go. Sometimes all you can do is jump into the well and hope for the best.

Thank you for the Patreon support that changed this from being a languishing project I had no idea what to do with, into something people have read.

Thank you to Tom for the cover art, and Becca for the generous loan of your face. Thank you Mark for helping with the making it printable, a process that generally terrifies me.

Huge thanks to Bookends, a bookshop that no longer exists in Gloucester, but was there in my teens and became the bookshop that lives in my head.